BEAN DOG

and

NUGGET

The Cookie

Charise Mericle Harper

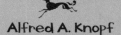

Alfred A. Knopf

THIS IS A BORZOI BOOK PUBLISHED BY ALFRED A. KNOPF

Copyright © 2013 by Charise Mericle Harper
All rights reserved. Published in the United States by Alfred A. Knopf, an imprint of Random House Children's Books,
a division of Random House, Inc., New York.
Knopf, Borzoi Books, and the colophon are registered trademarks of Random House, Inc.
Visit us on the Web! randomhouse.com/kids
Educators and librarians, for a variety of teaching tools, visit us at RHTeachersLibrarians.com
Library of Congress Cataloging-in-Publication Data
Harper, Charise Mericle.
Bean Dog and Nugget : the cookie / Charise Mericle Harper. — 1st ed.
   p.   cm.— (Bean Dog and Nugget)
Summary: Bean Dog and Nugget argue about who will get the bigger half
of a cookie. They try to outwit each other by all sorts of imaginative
means—but they find out that what really counts in the end is friendship.
ISBN 978-0-307-97710-6 (pbk.) — ISBN 978-0-307-97711-3 (lib. bdg.) — ISBN 978-0-307-97712-0 (ebook)
1. Graphic novels. [1. Graphic novels. 2. Sharing—Fiction.
3. Friendship—Fiction. 4. Humorous stories.] I. Title.
PZ7.7.H37Bef 2013
2012029374

The text of this book is set in 16-point Matt Md Text.
The illustrations were created using digital coloring.

MANUFACTURED IN MALAYSIA
May 2013   10 9 8 7 6 5 4 3 2 1   First Edition

Random House Children's Books supports the
First Amendment and celebrates the right to read.

For Luther and Henry,
two boys who like cookies

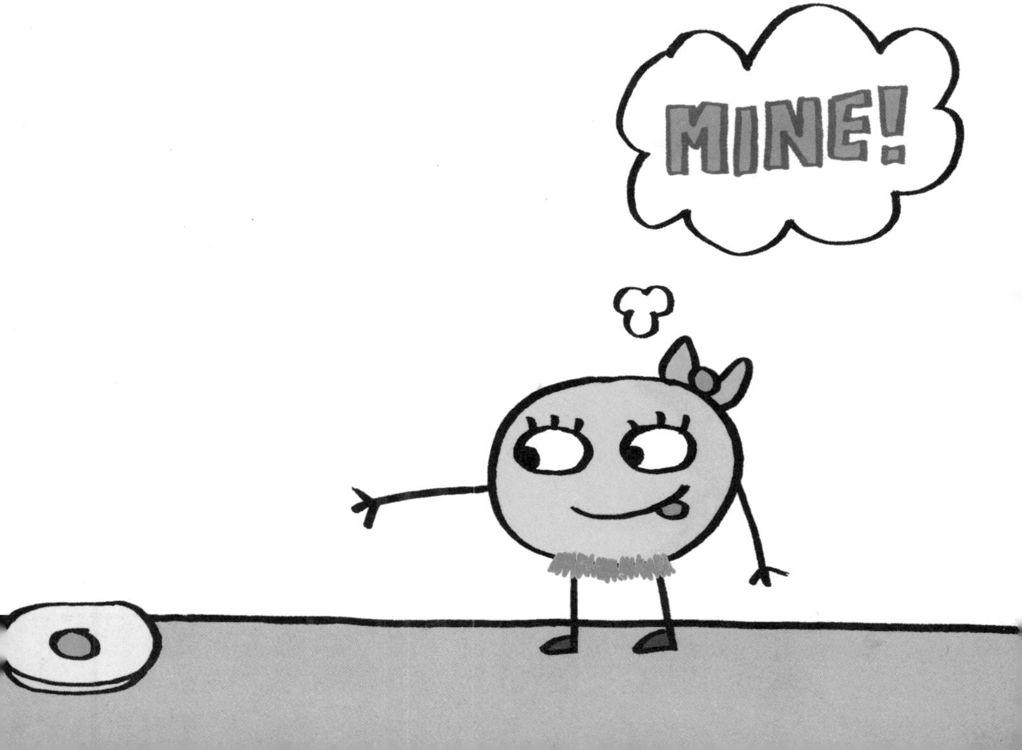
MINE!

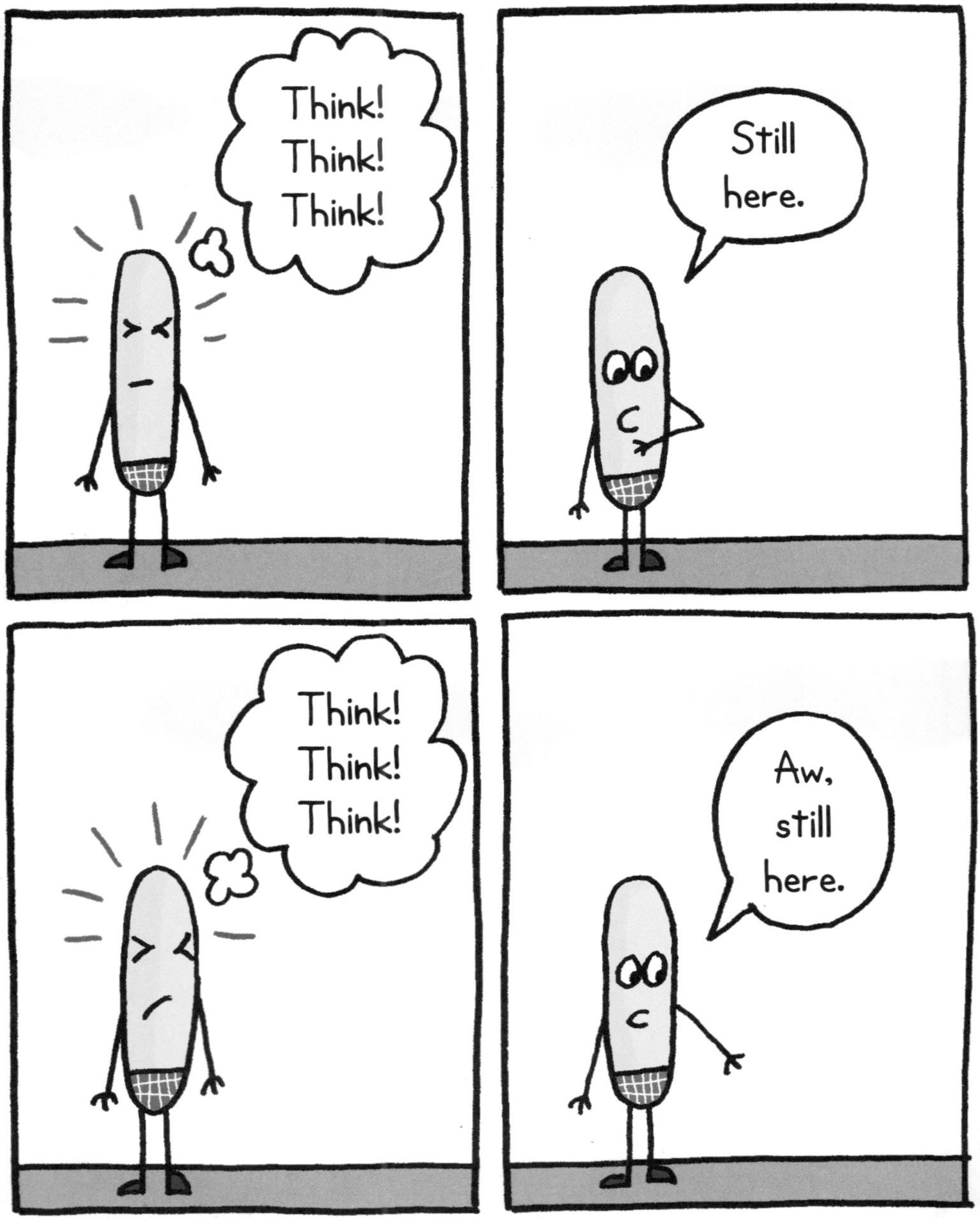
Think! Think! Think!
Still here.
Think! Think! Think!
Aw, still here.

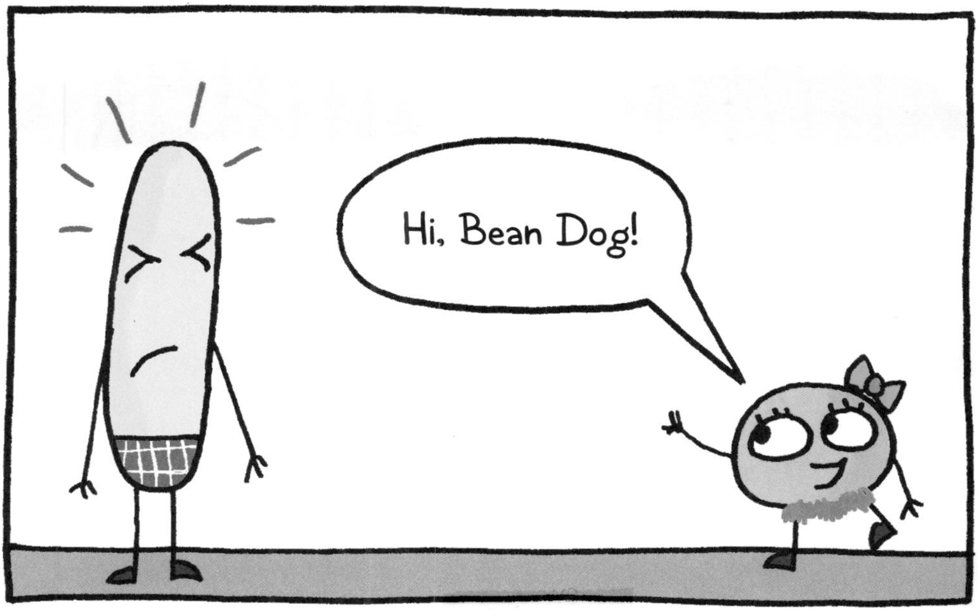
Hi, Bean Dog!

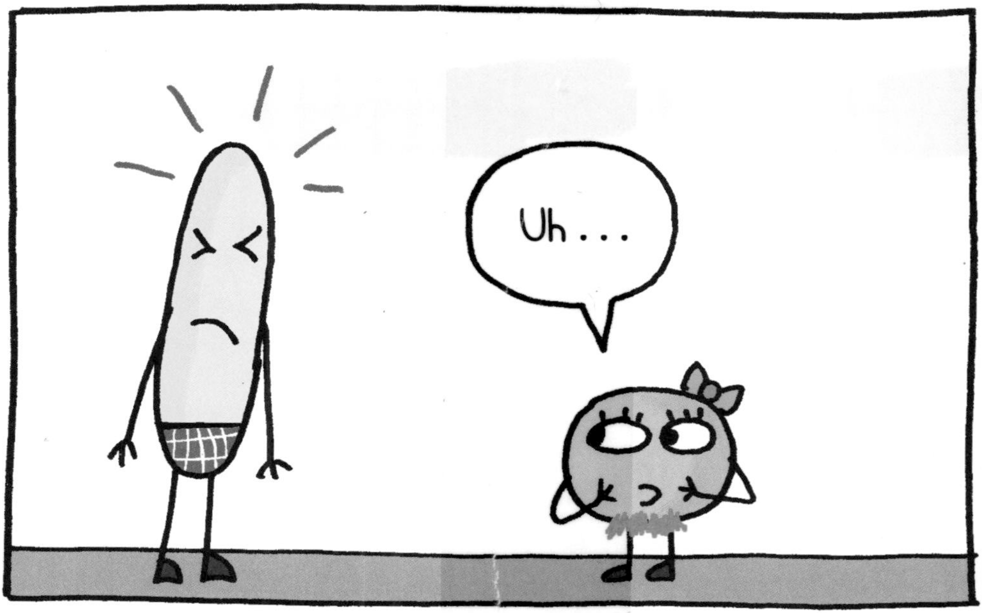
Uh . . .

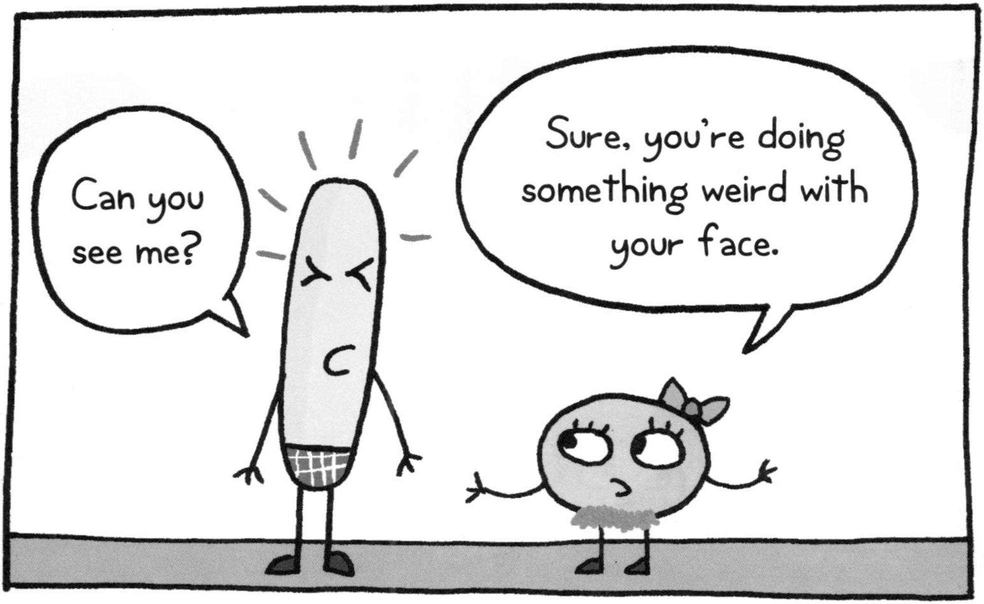
Can you see me?
Sure, you're doing something weird with your face.

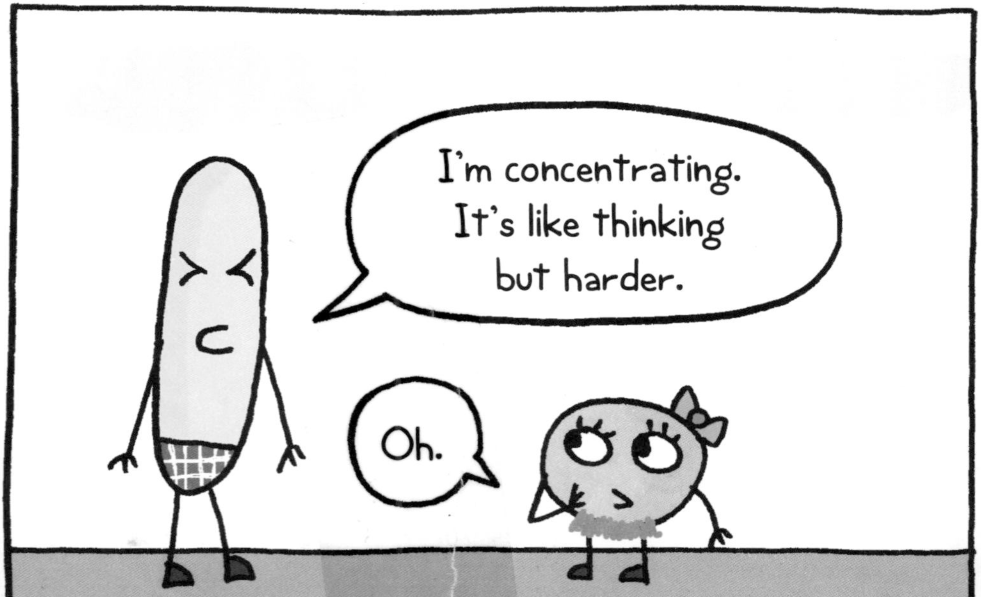
I'm concentrating. It's like thinking but harder.
Oh.

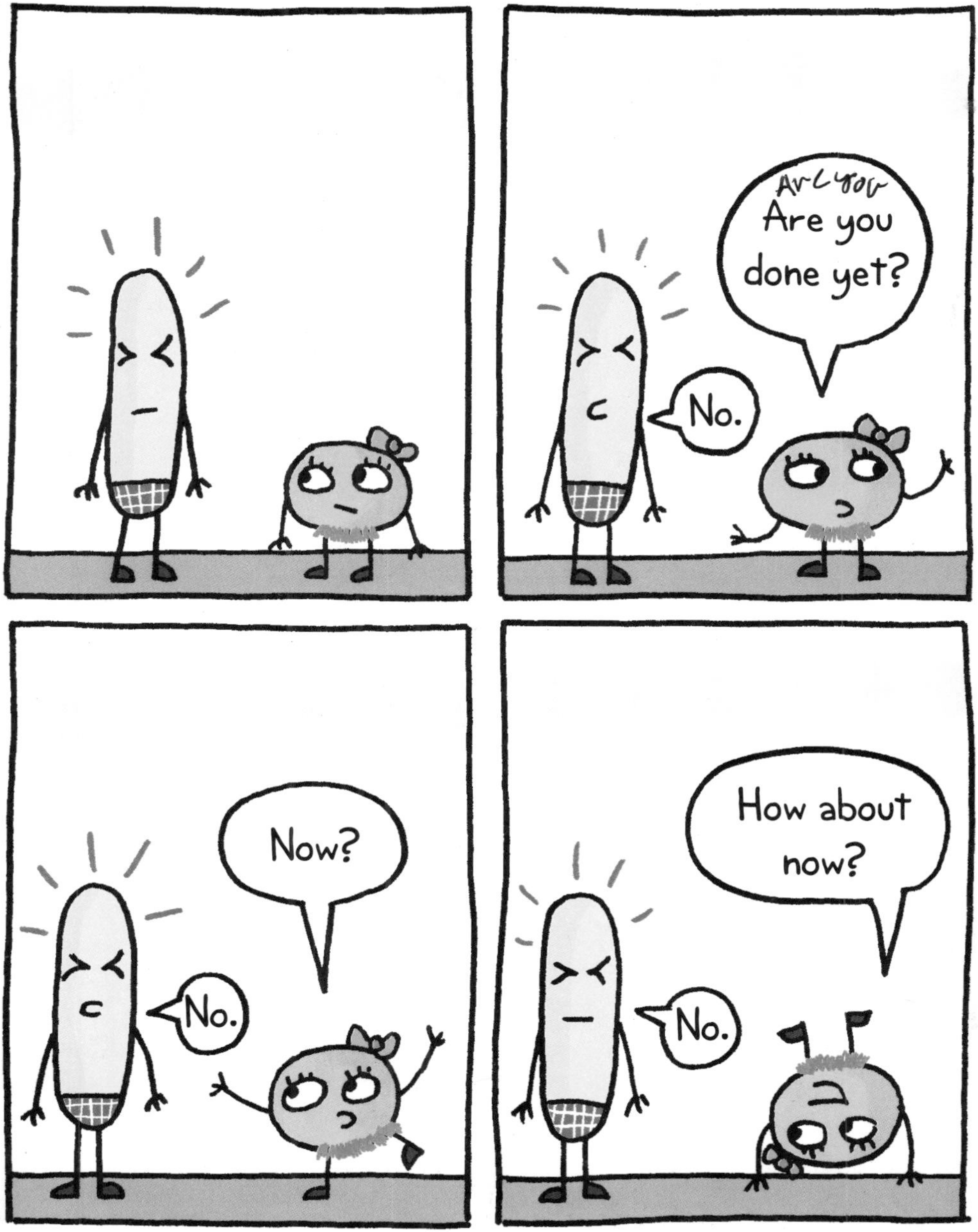
Are you done yet?
No.
Now?
No.
How about now?
No.

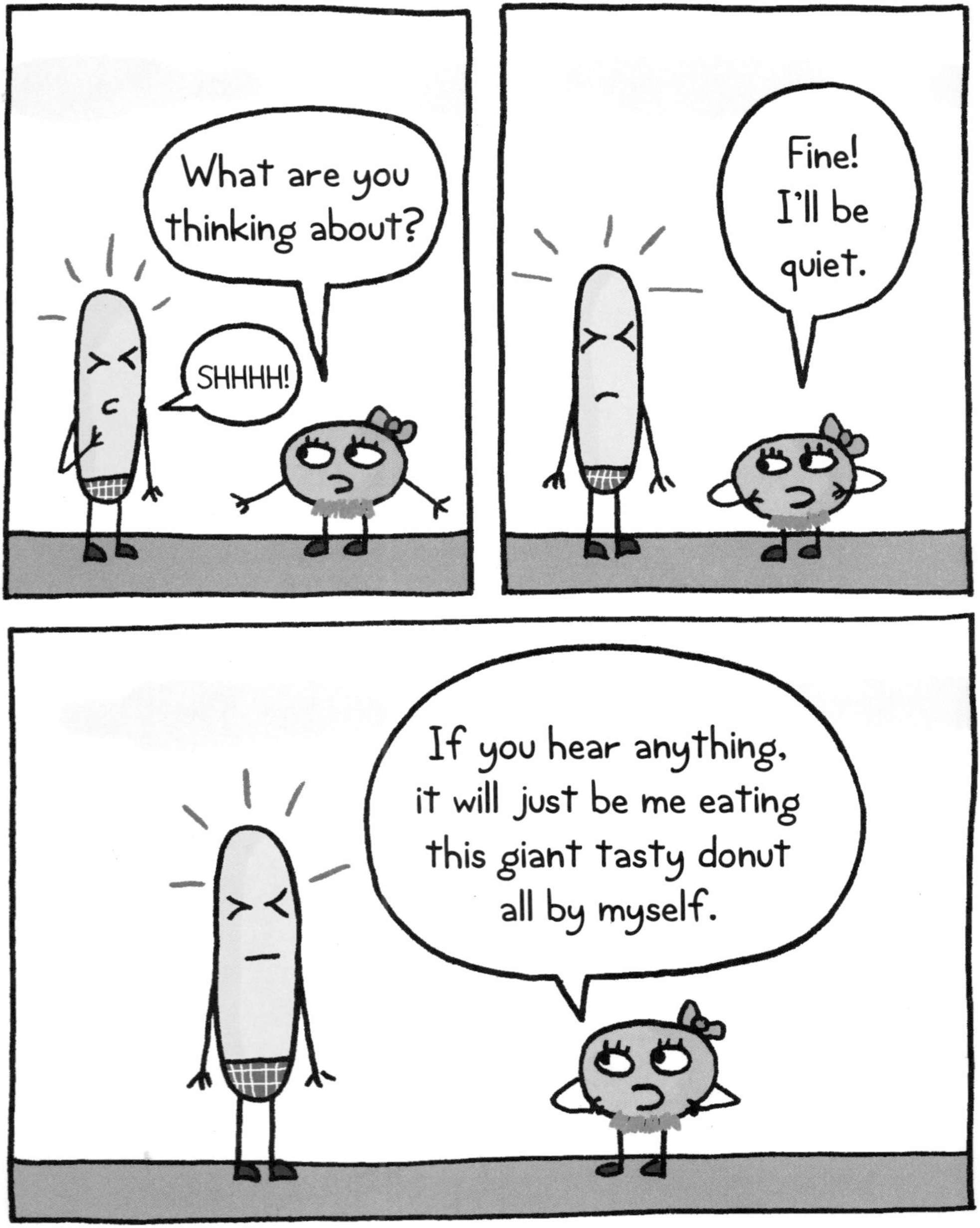
What are you thinking about?
SHHHH!
Fine! I'll be quiet.
If you hear anything, it will just be me eating this giant tasty donut all by myself.

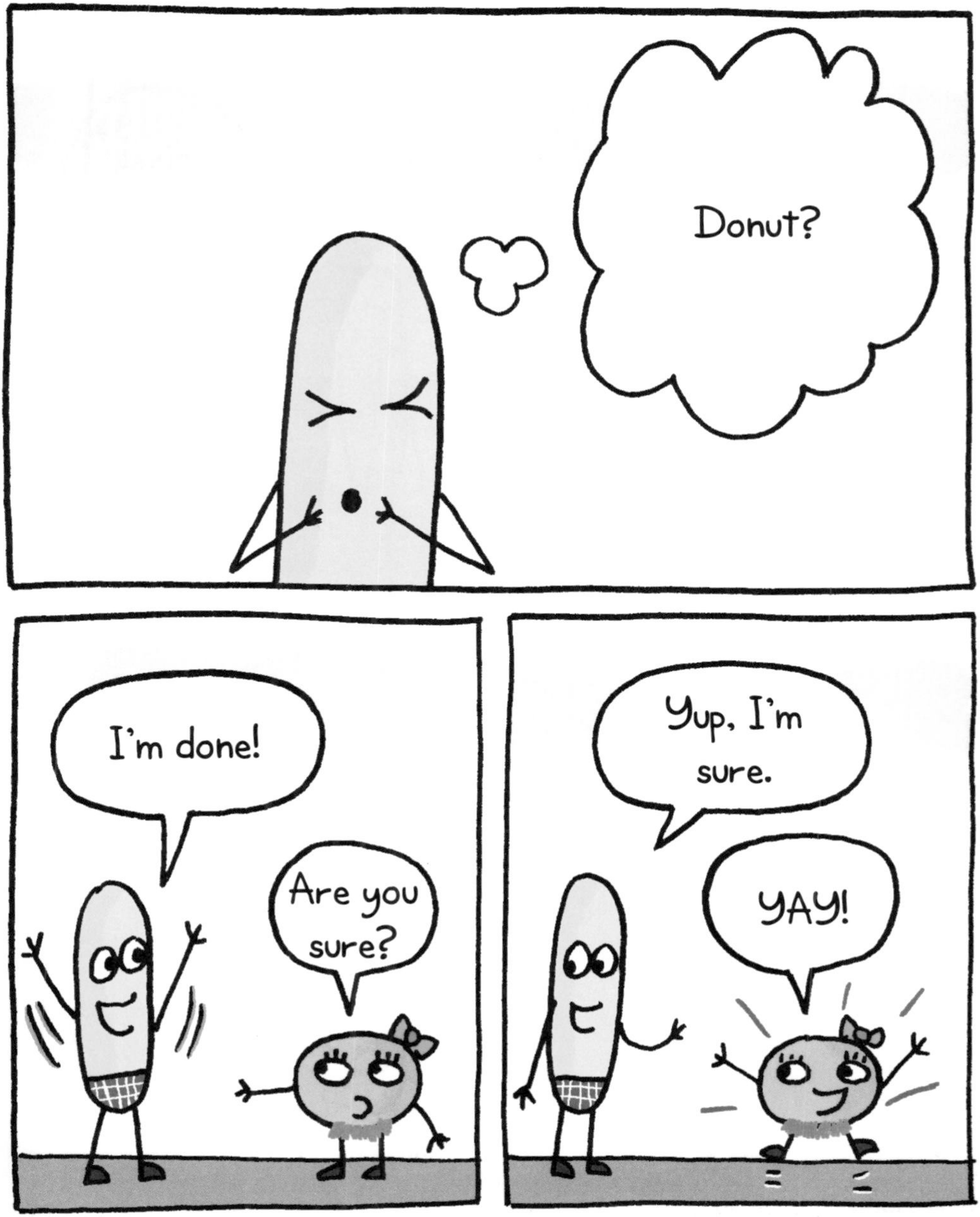
Donut?
I'm done!
Are you sure?
Yup, I'm sure.
YAY!

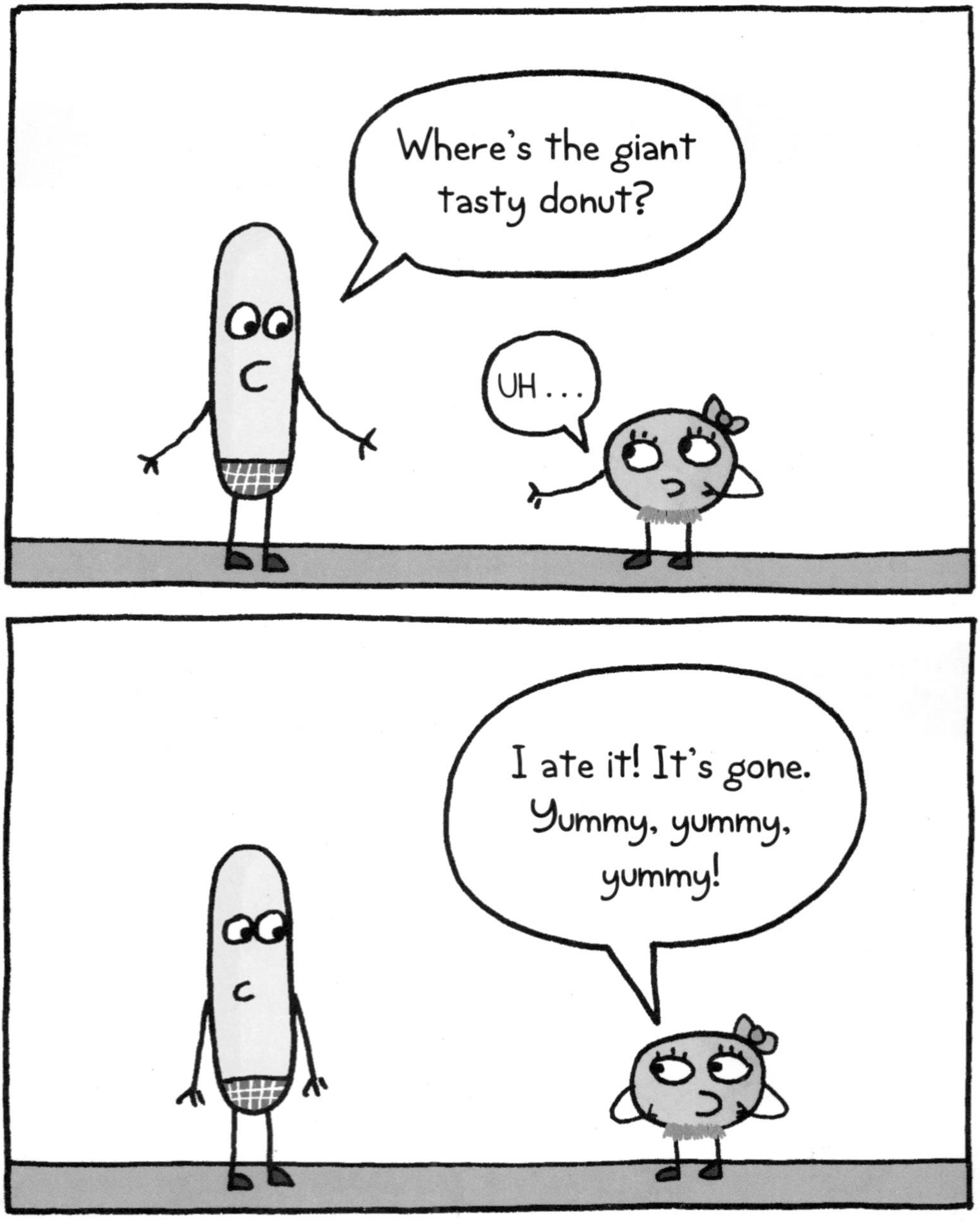
Where's the giant tasty donut?
UH . . .
I ate it! It's gone. Yummy, yummy, yummy!

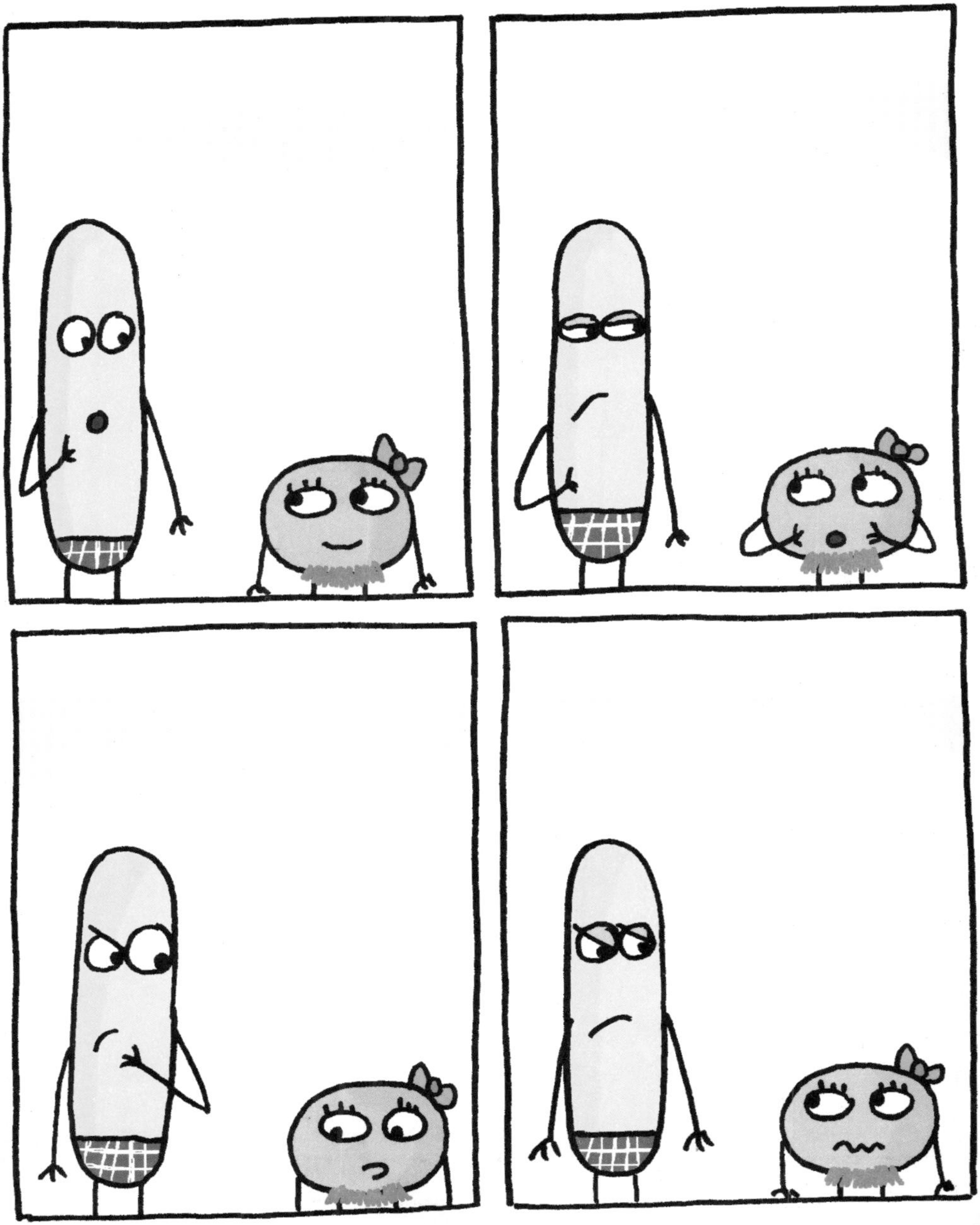

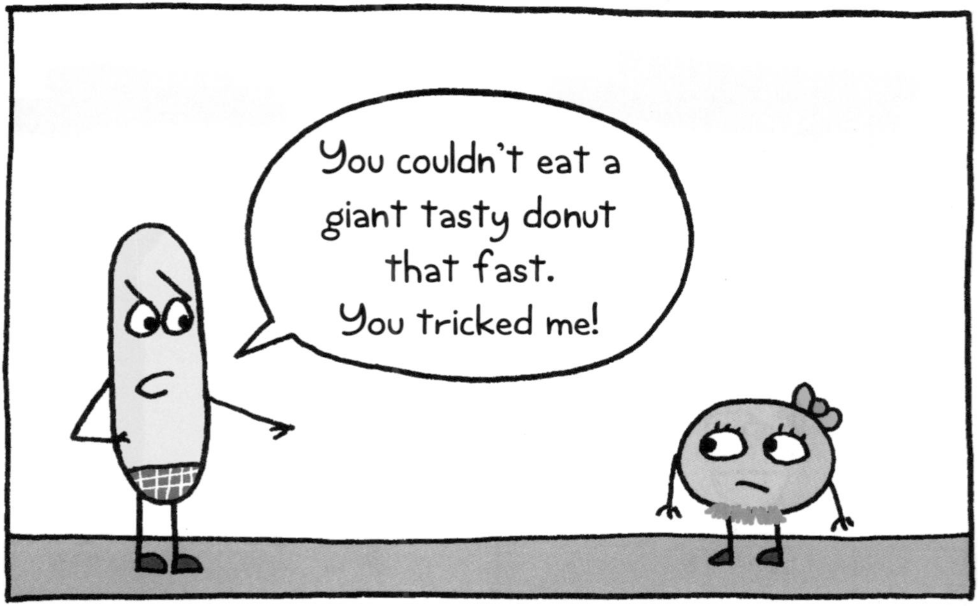
You couldn't eat a giant tasty donut that fast. You tricked me!

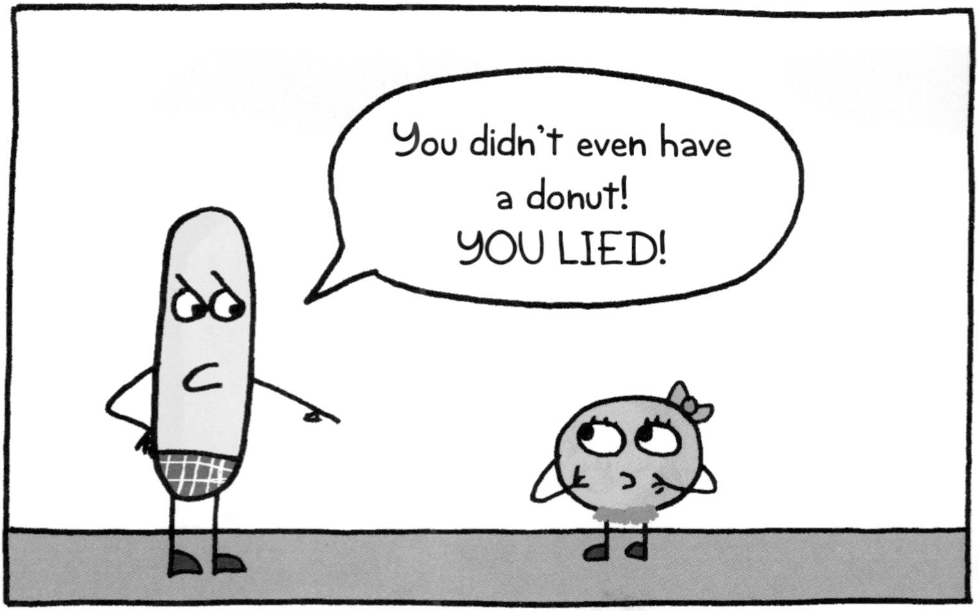
You didn't even have a donut! YOU LIED!

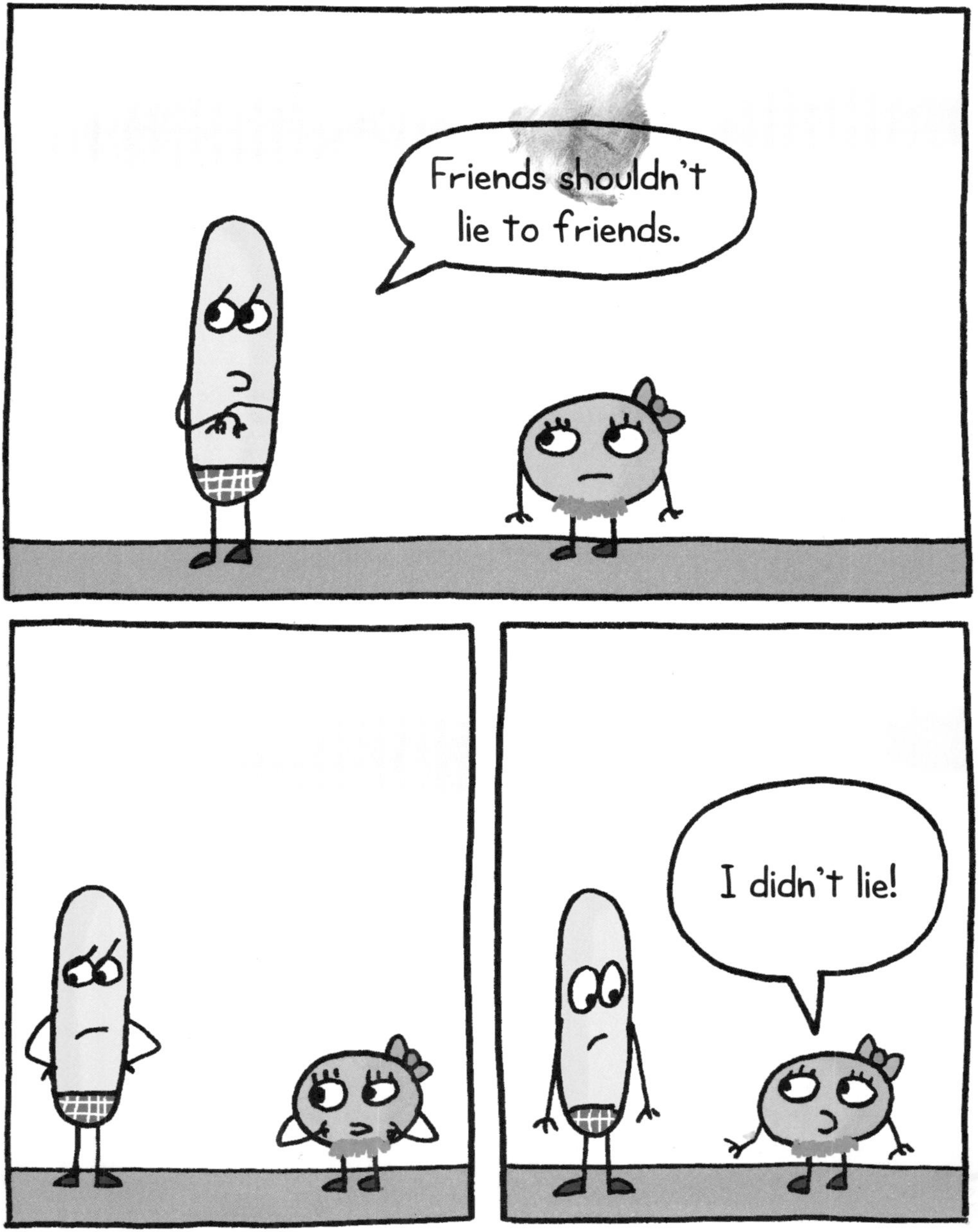
Friends shouldn't lie to friends.
I didn't lie!

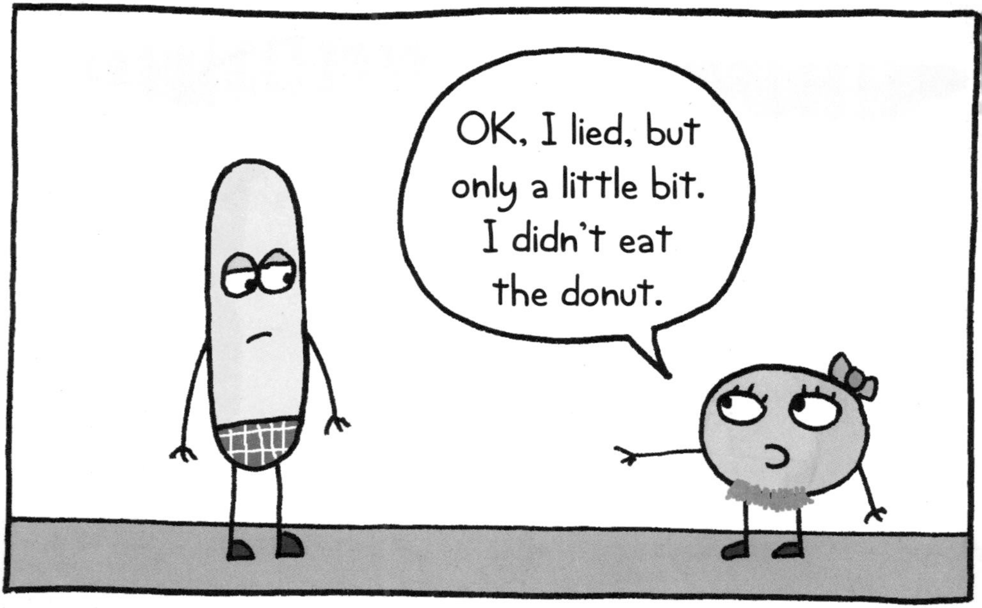
OK, I lied, but only a little bit. I didn't eat the donut.

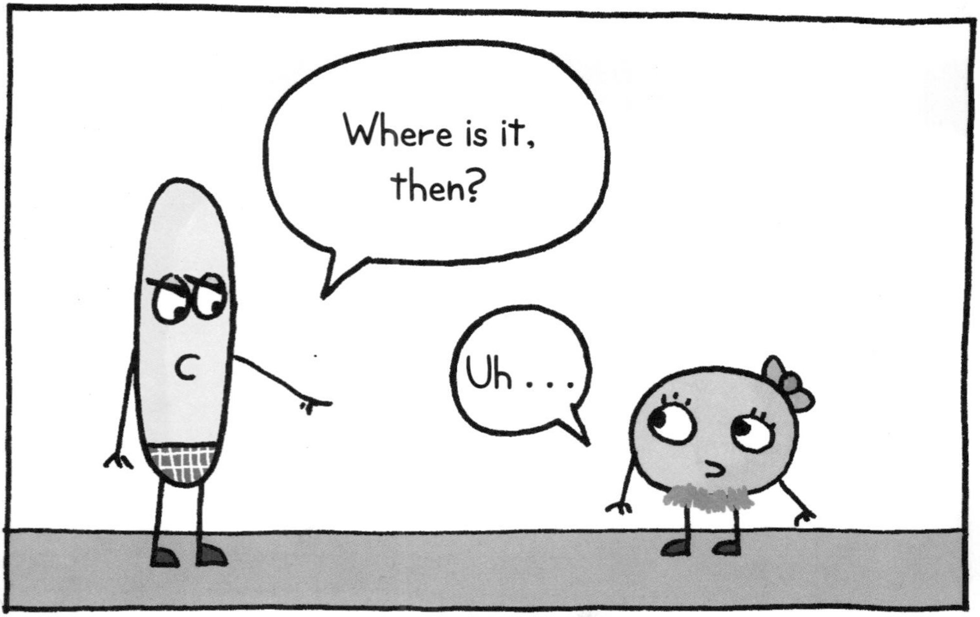
Where is it, then?
Uh . . .

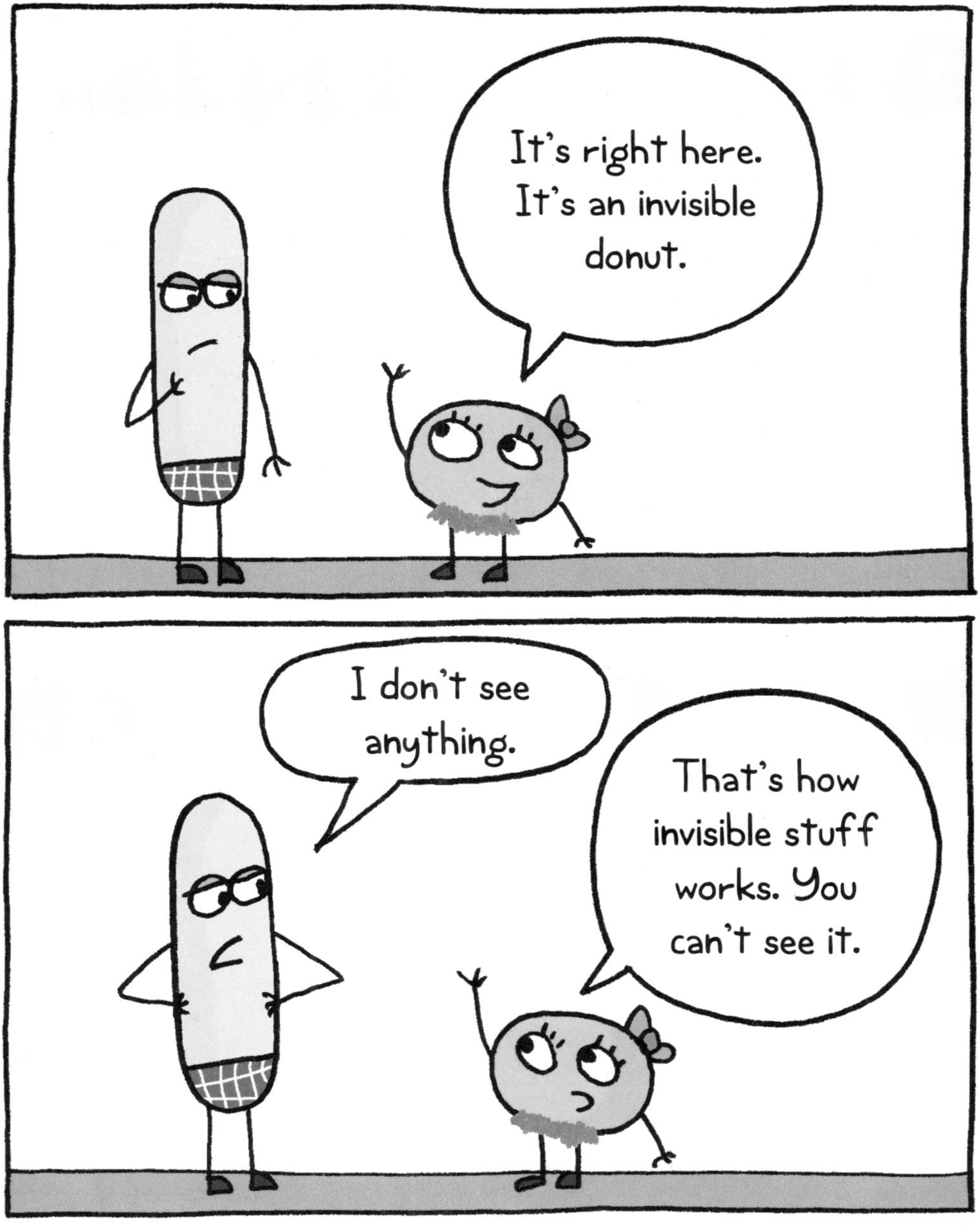
It's right here. It's an invisible donut.
I don't see anything.
That's how invisible stuff works. You can't see it.

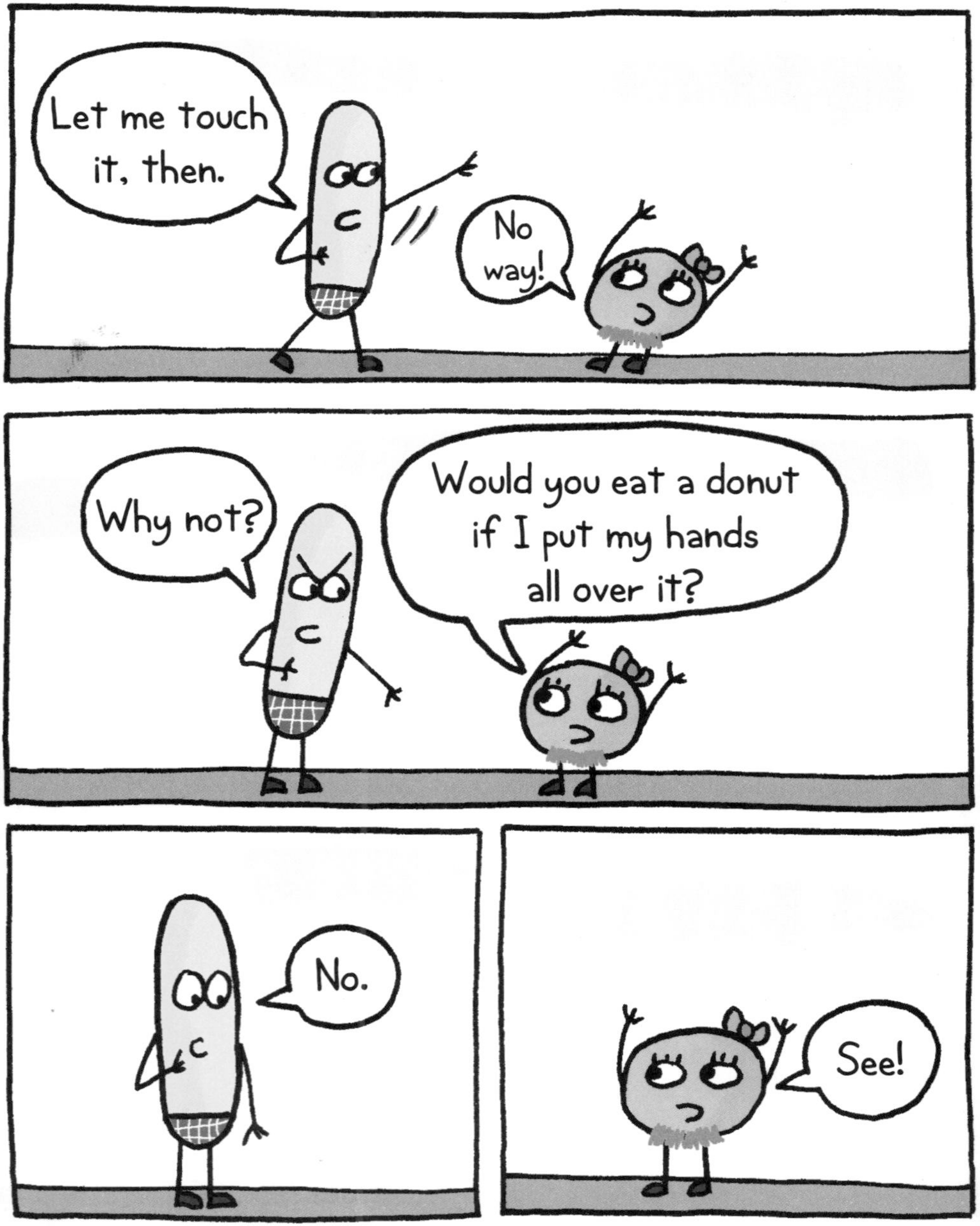
Let me touch it, then.
No way!
Why not?
Would you eat a donut if I put my hands all over it?
No.
See!

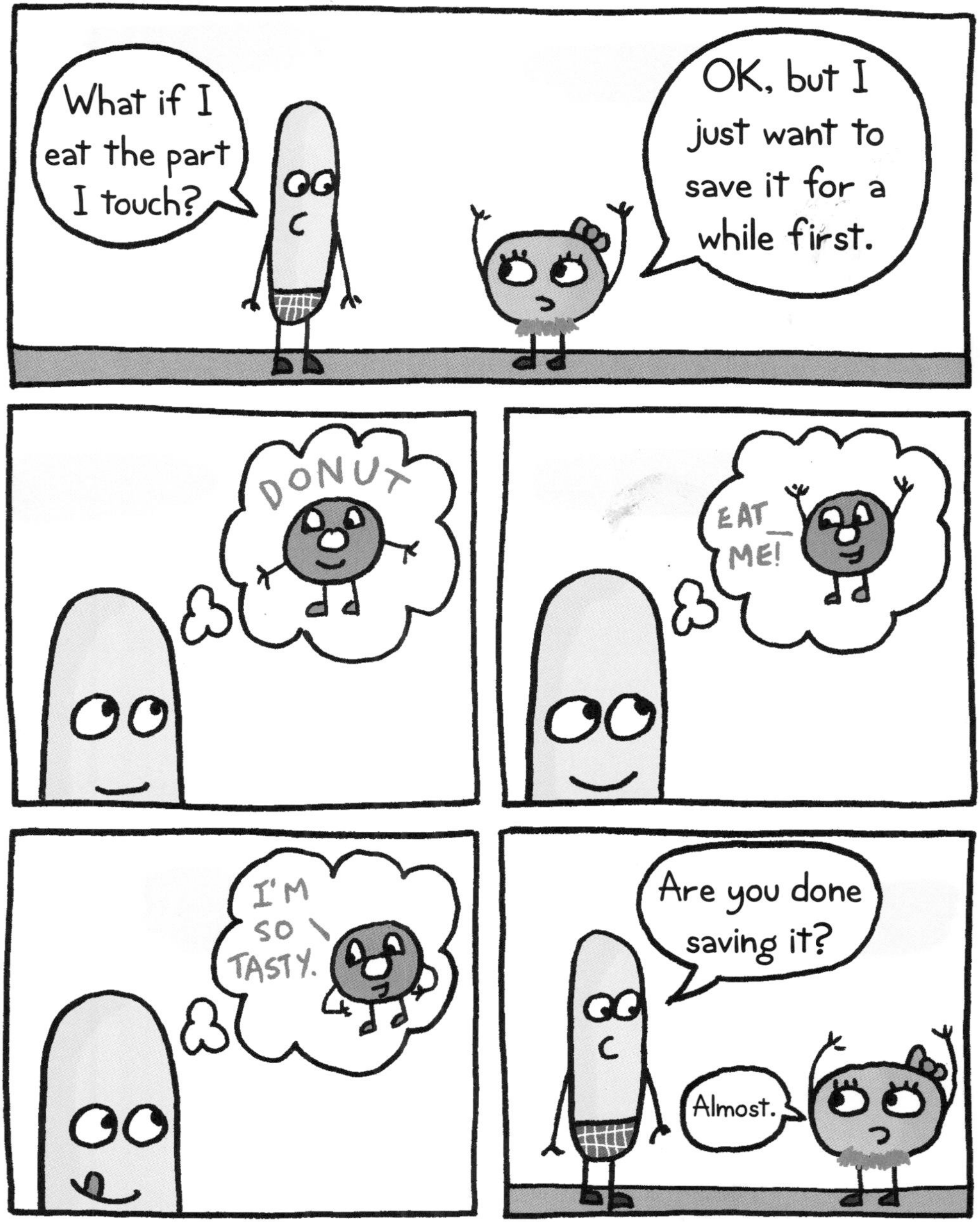
What if I eat the part I touch?
OK, but I just want to save it for a while first.
DONUT
EAT ME!
I'M SO TASTY.
Are you done saving it?
Almost.

I want to show you some cool donut tricks first.
OK.
The one-hand, one-leg catch.
Did you catch it?
Yup, it's right here.
This next one is really good.

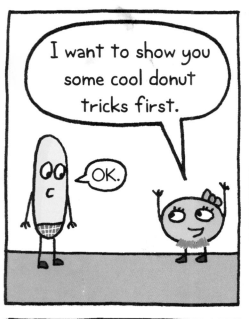

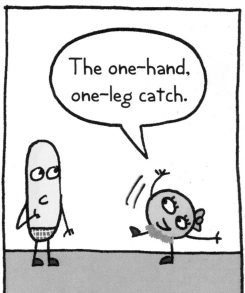

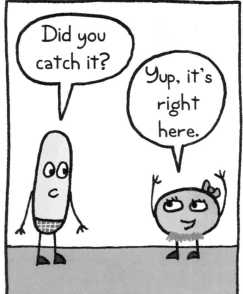

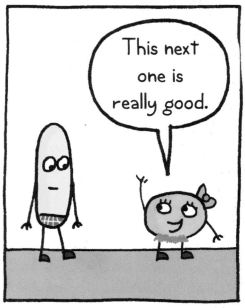

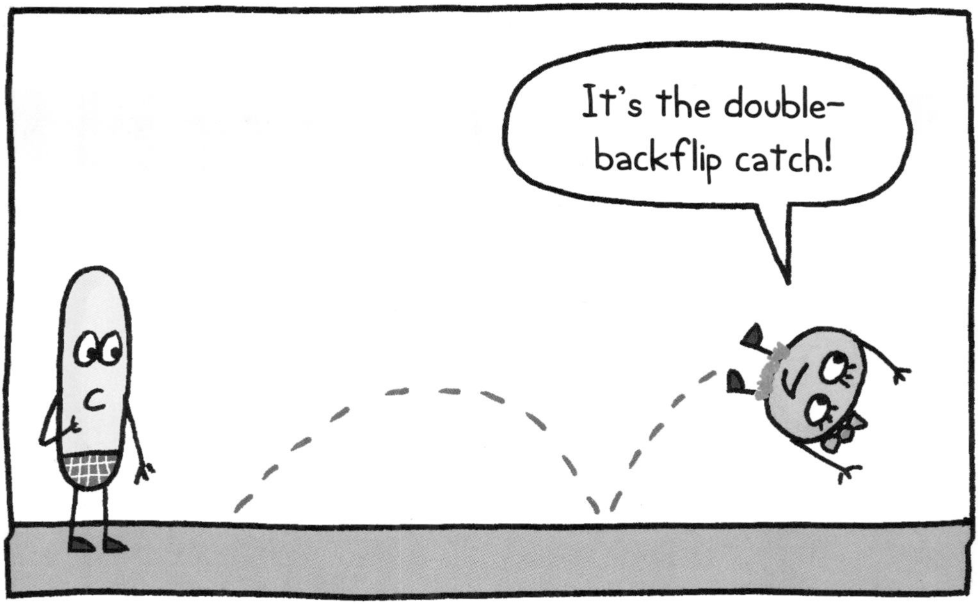
It's the double-
backflip catch!

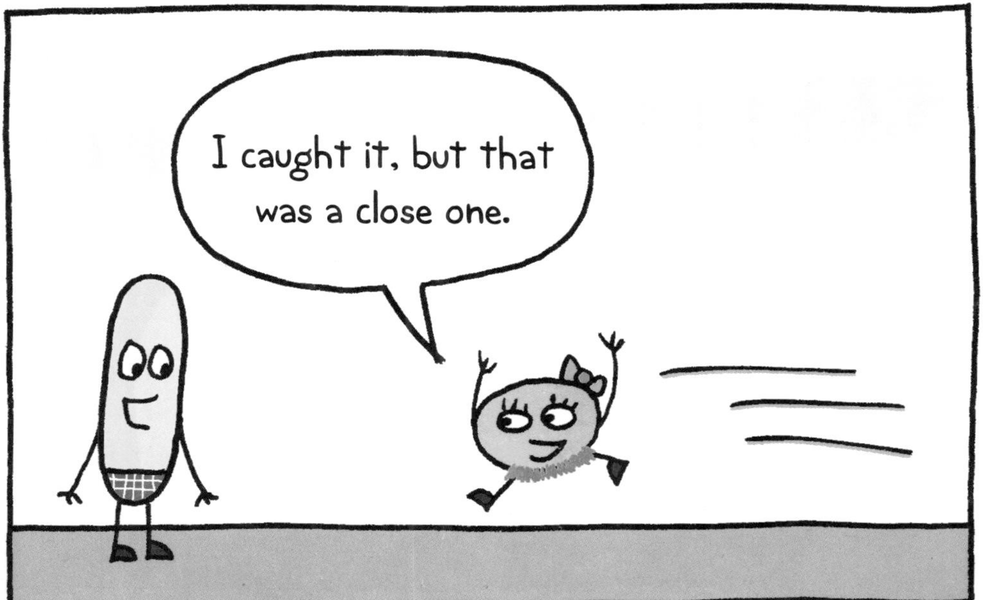
I caught it, but that
was a close one.

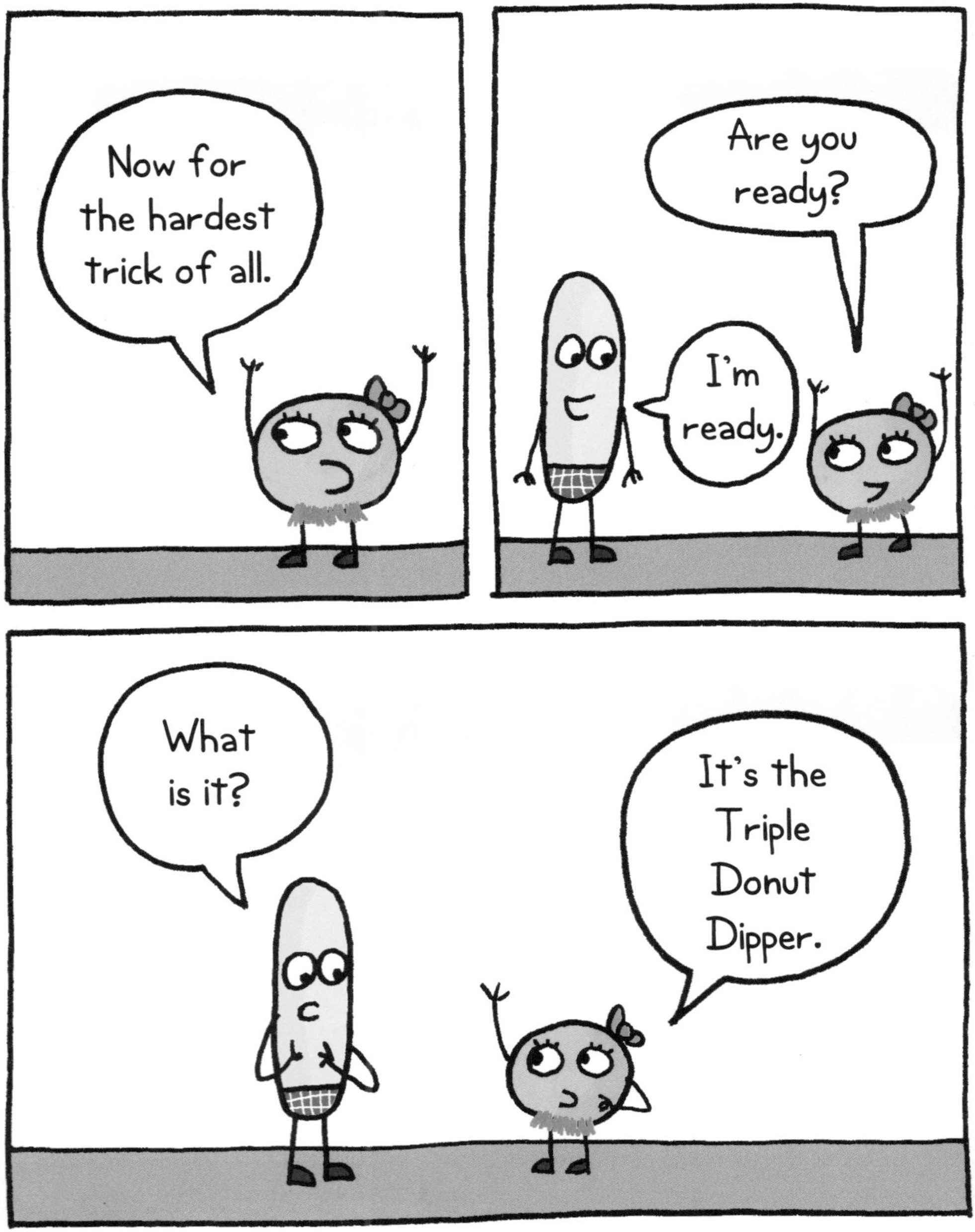
Now for the hardest trick of all.
Are you ready?
I'm ready.
What is it?
It's the Triple Donut Dipper.

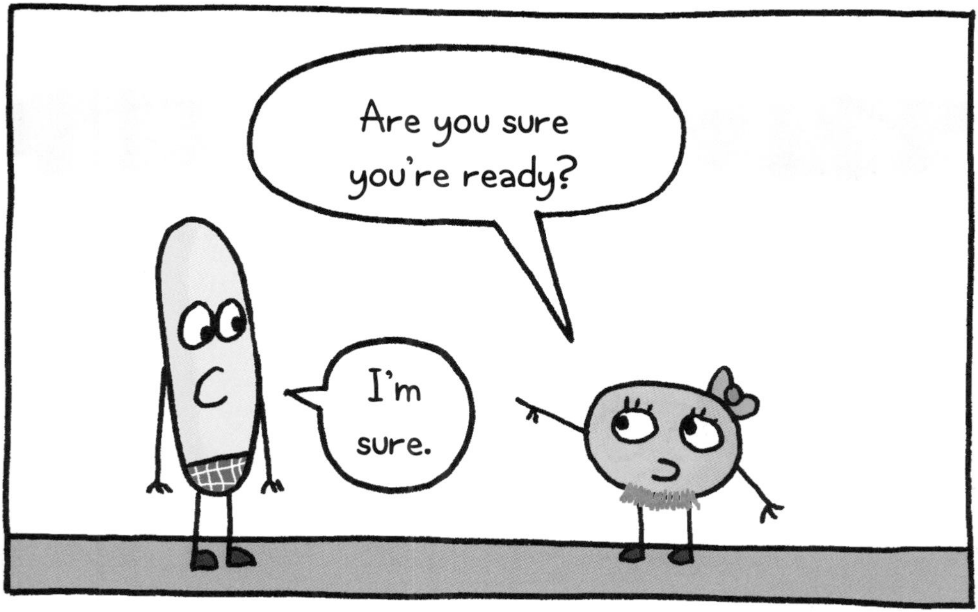
Are you sure you're ready?
I'm sure.

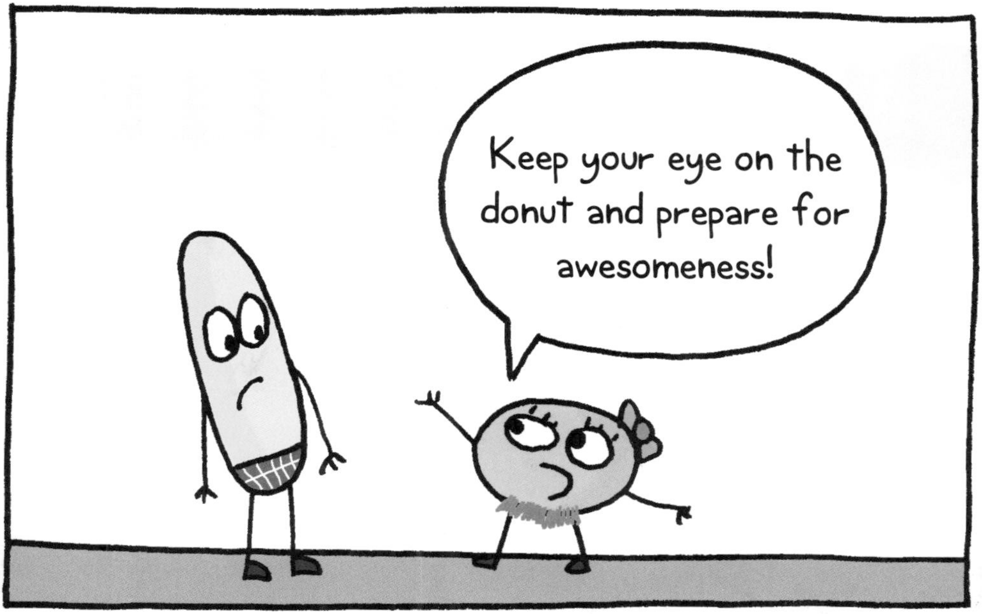
Keep your eye on the donut and prepare for awesomeness!

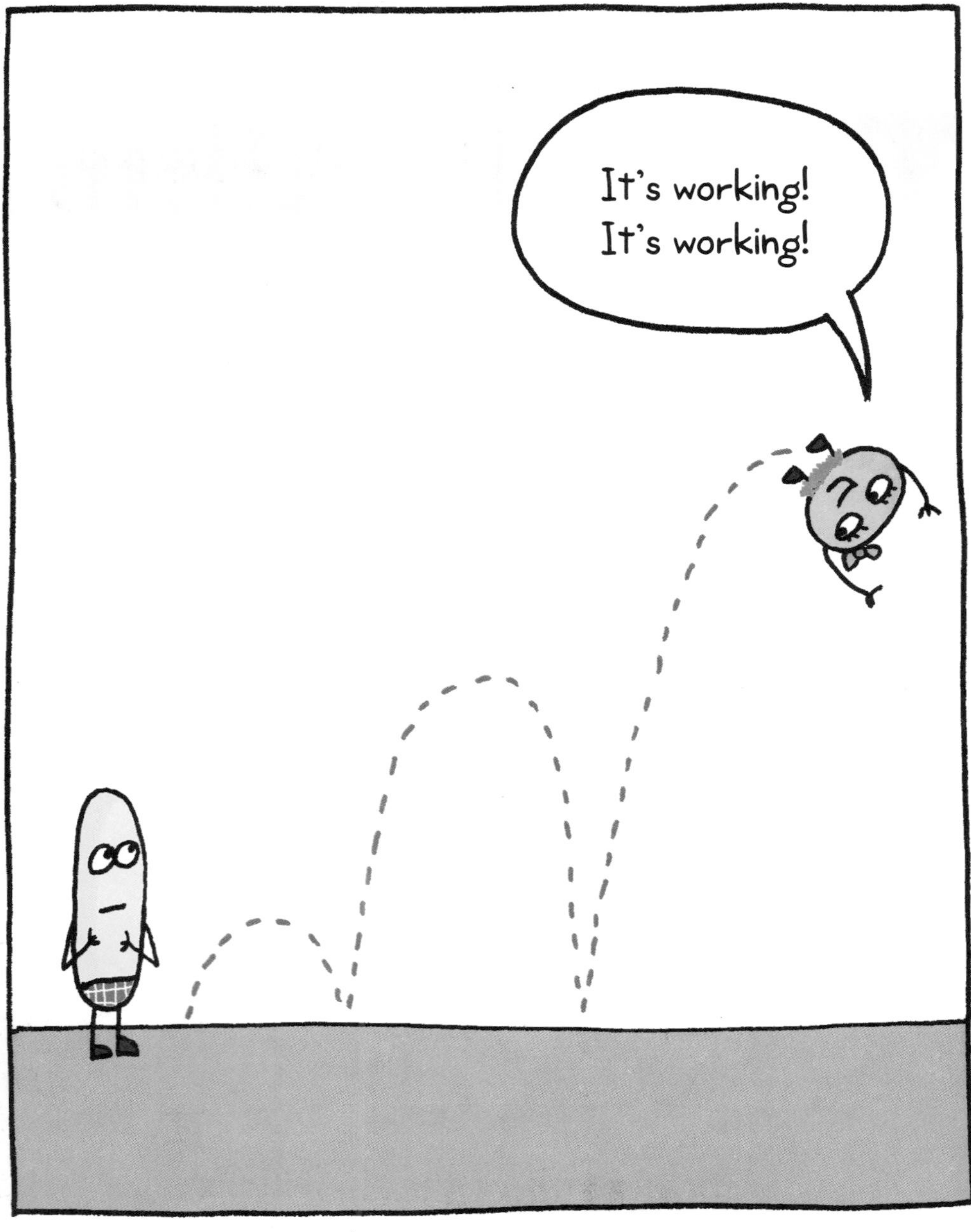
It's working!
It's working!

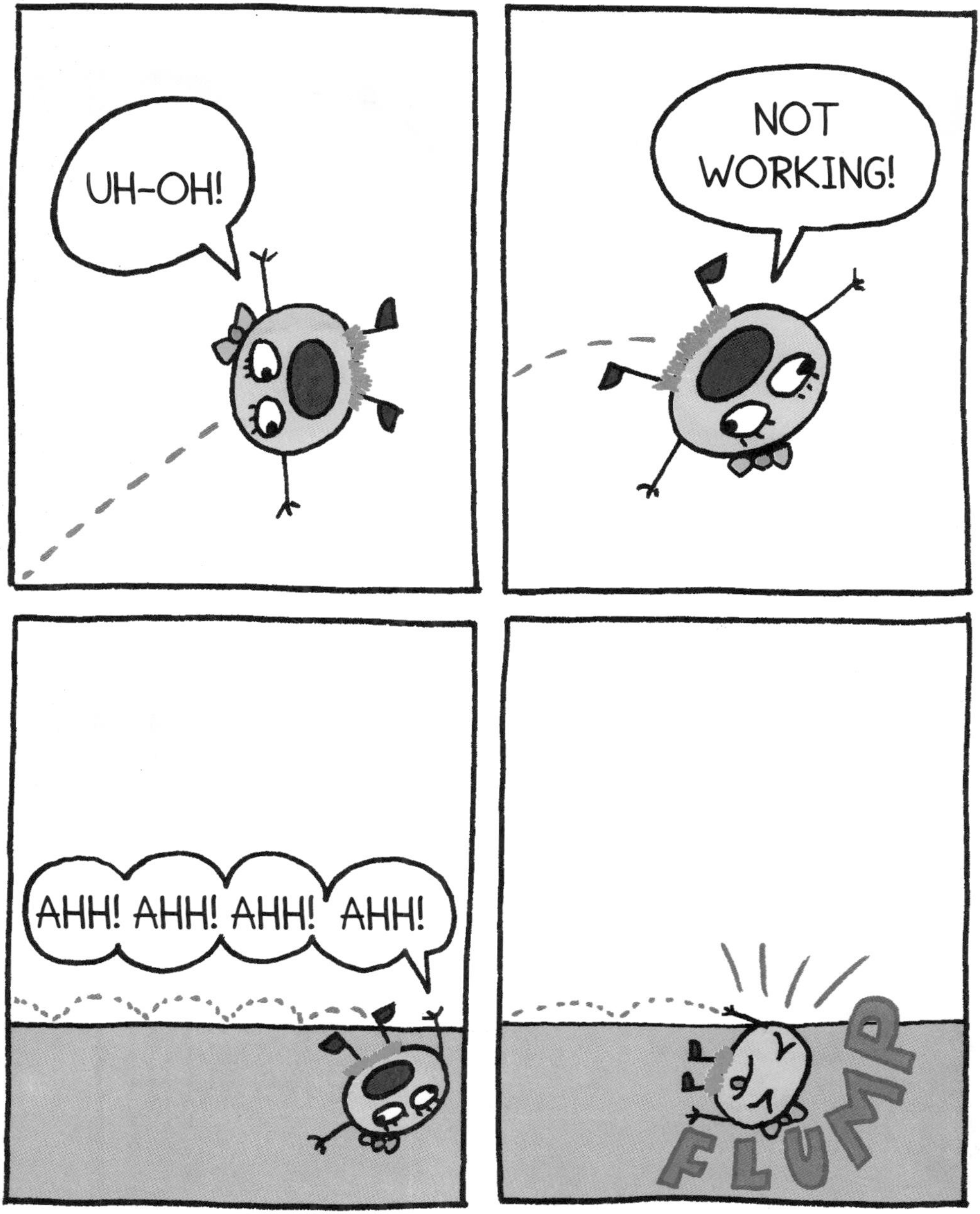
UH-OH!
NOT WORKING!
AHH! AHH! AHH! AHH!
FLUMP

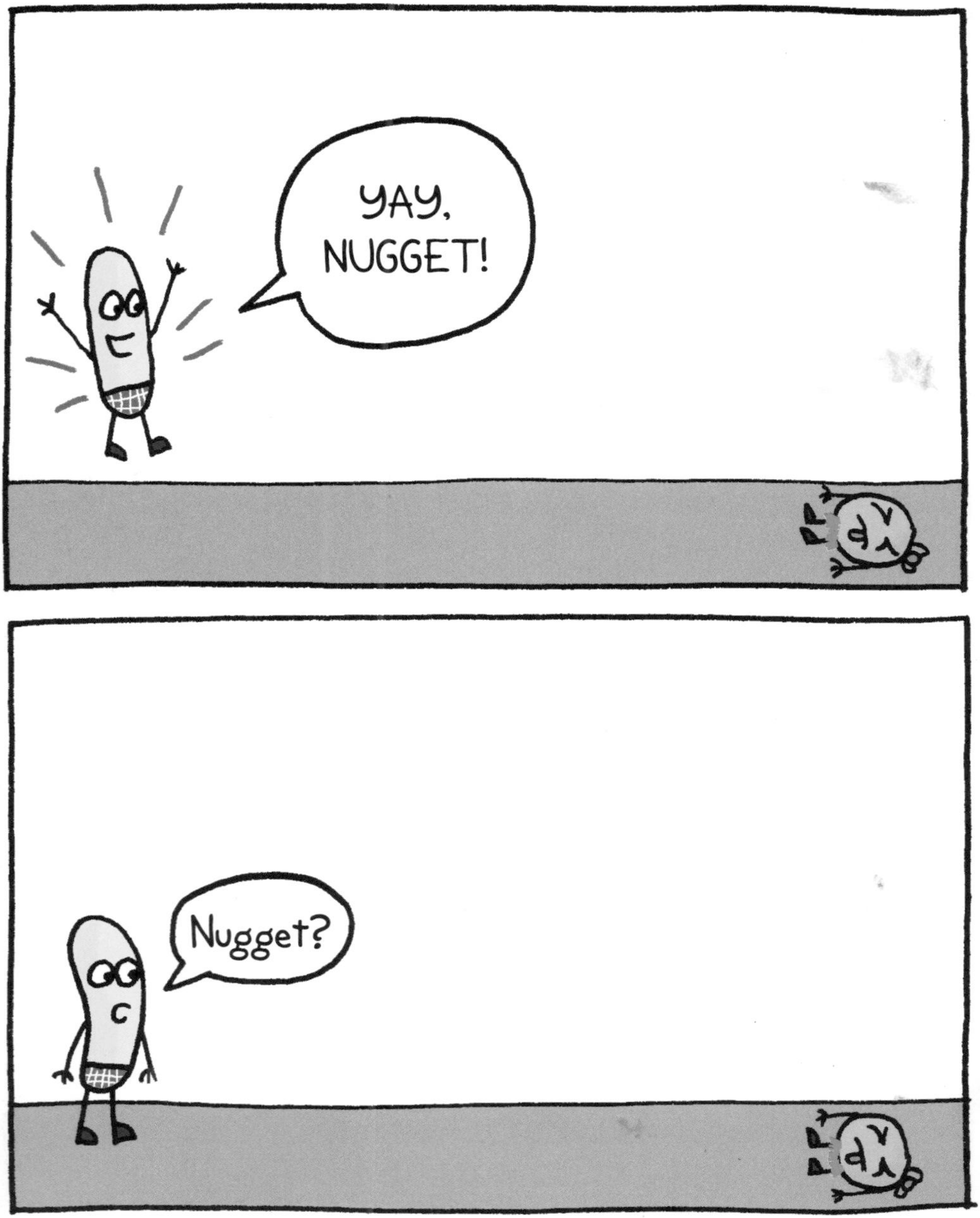
YAY, NUGGET!
Nugget?

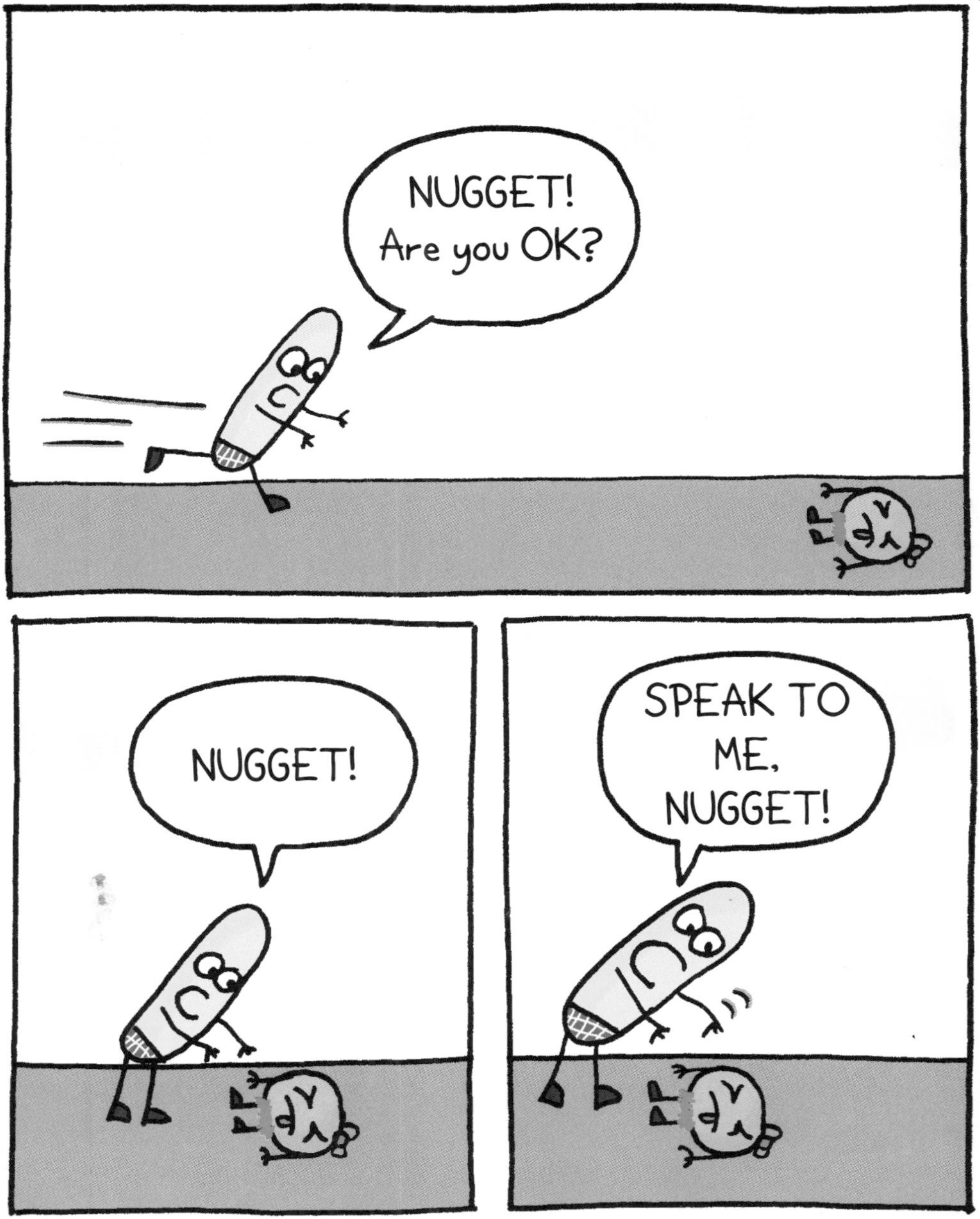
NUGGET! Are you OK?
NUGGET!
SPEAK TO ME, NUGGET!

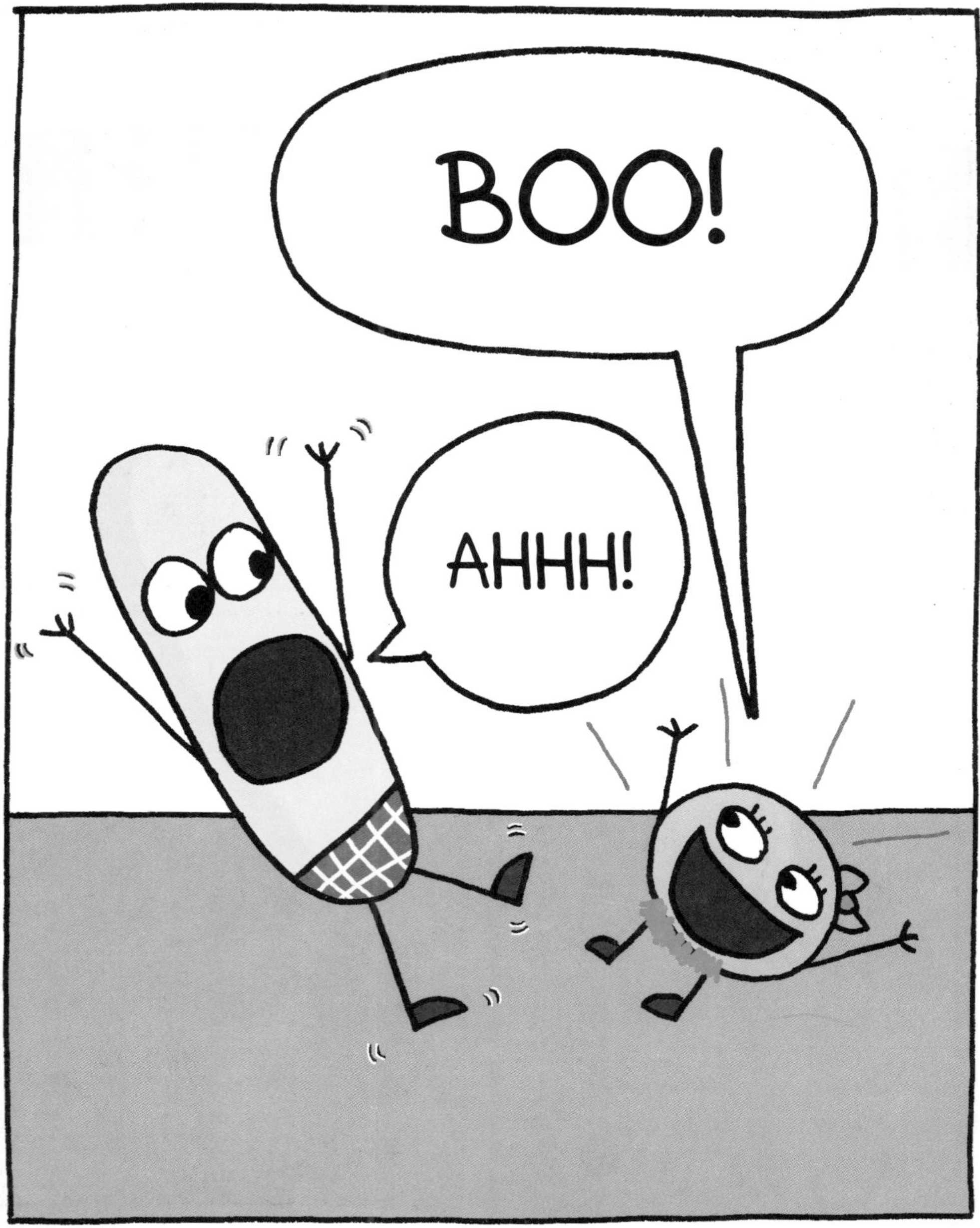
BOO!
AHHH!

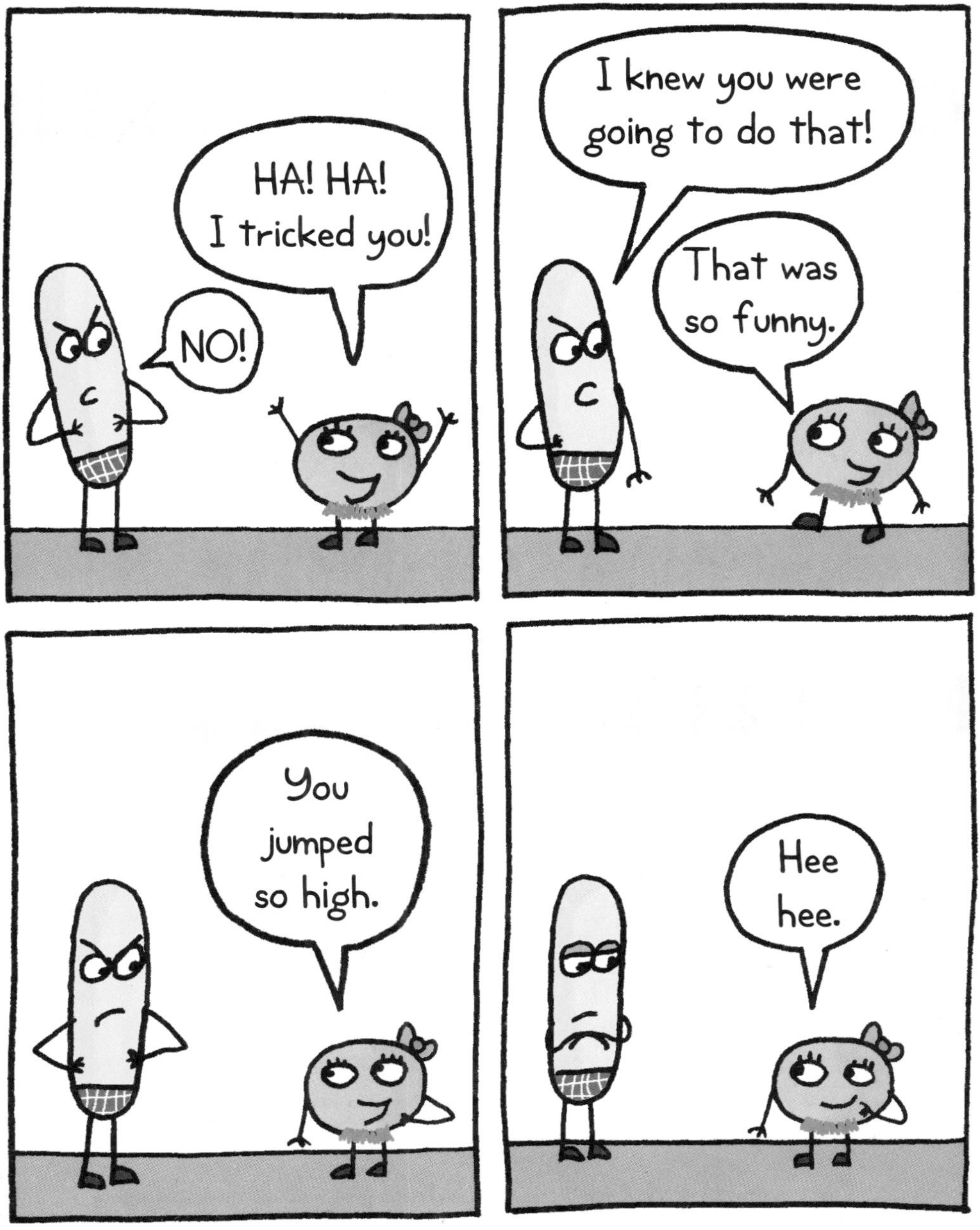
HA! HA!
I tricked you!
NO!
I knew you were going to do that!
That was so funny.
You jumped so high.
Hee hee.

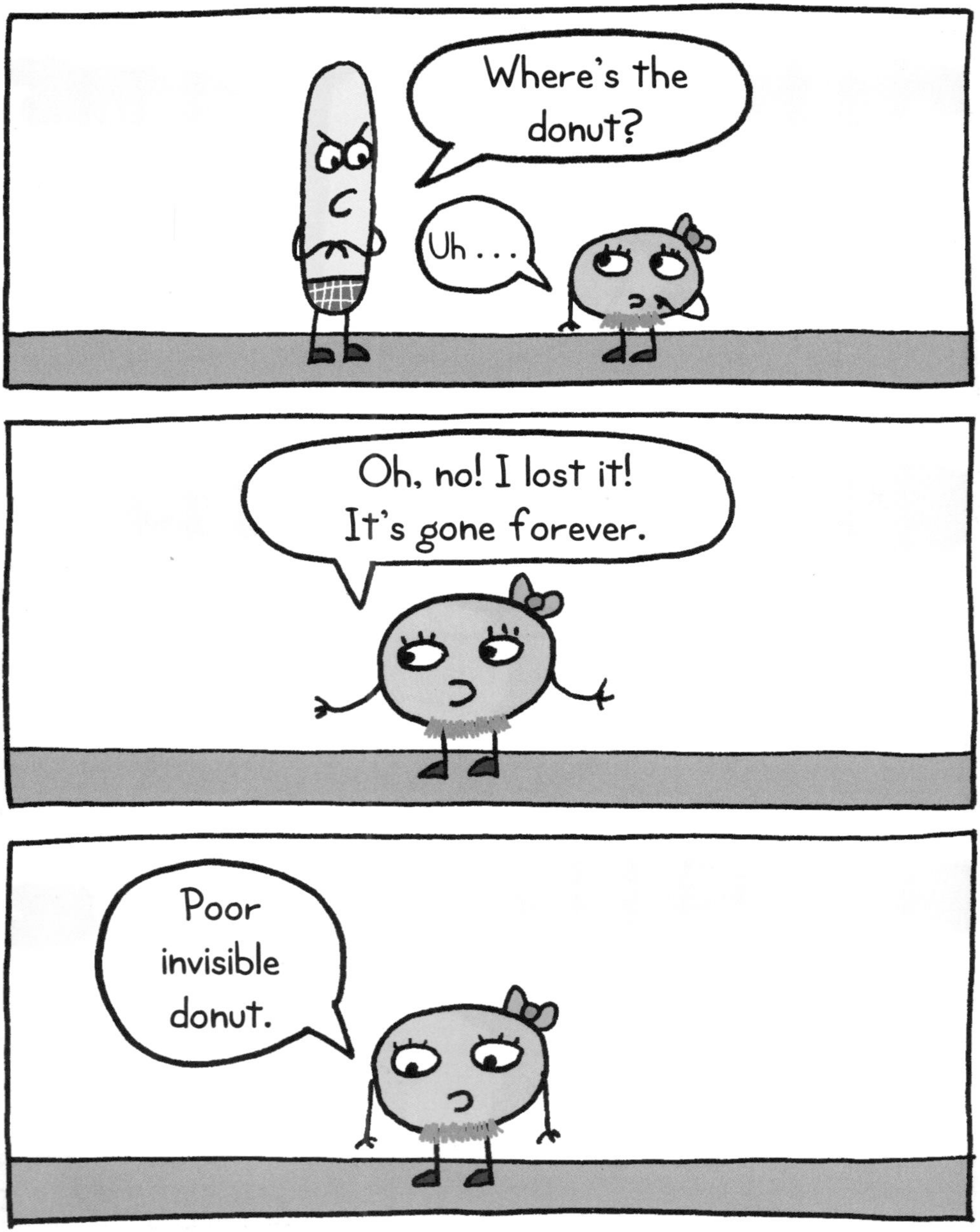
Where's the donut?
Uh . . .
Oh, no! I lost it! It's gone forever.
Poor invisible donut.

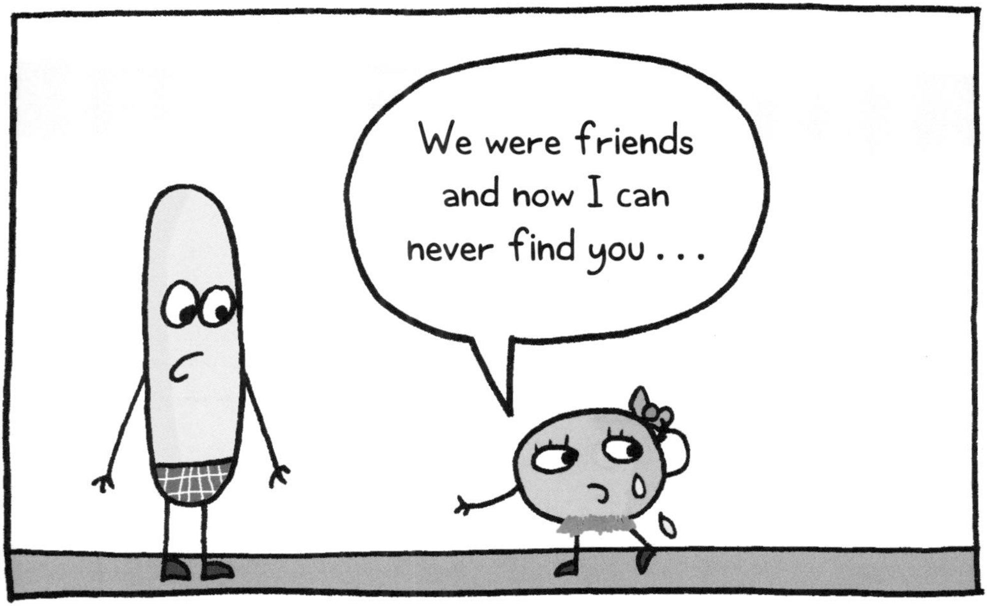
We were friends and now I can never find you . . .

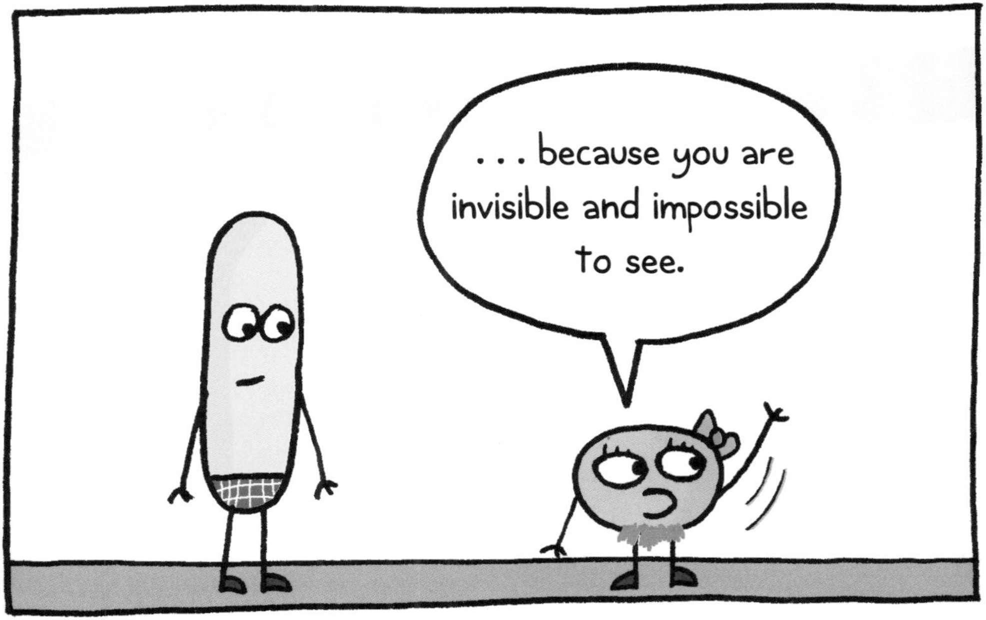
. . . because you are invisible and impossible to see.

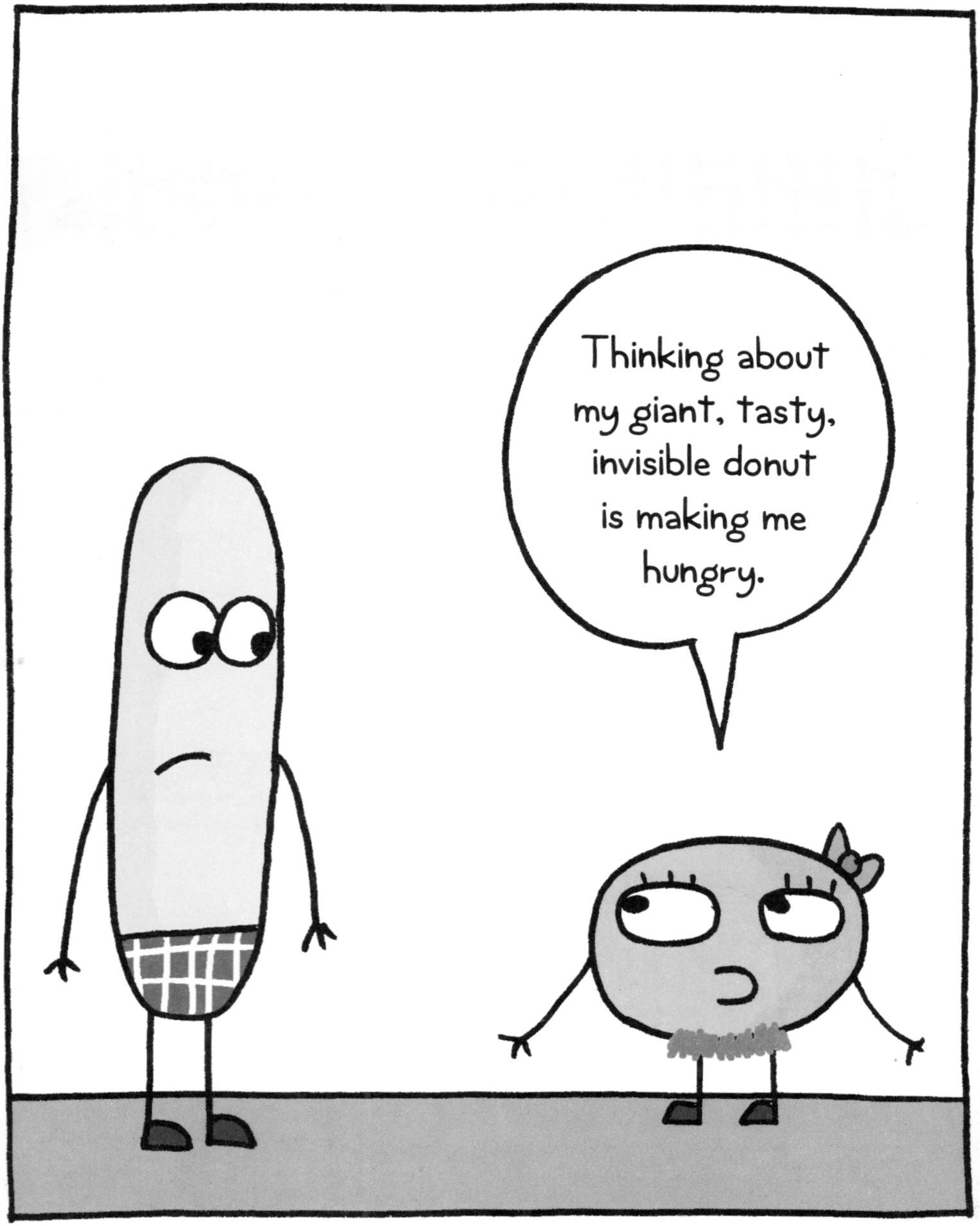
Thinking about my giant, tasty, invisible donut is making me hungry.

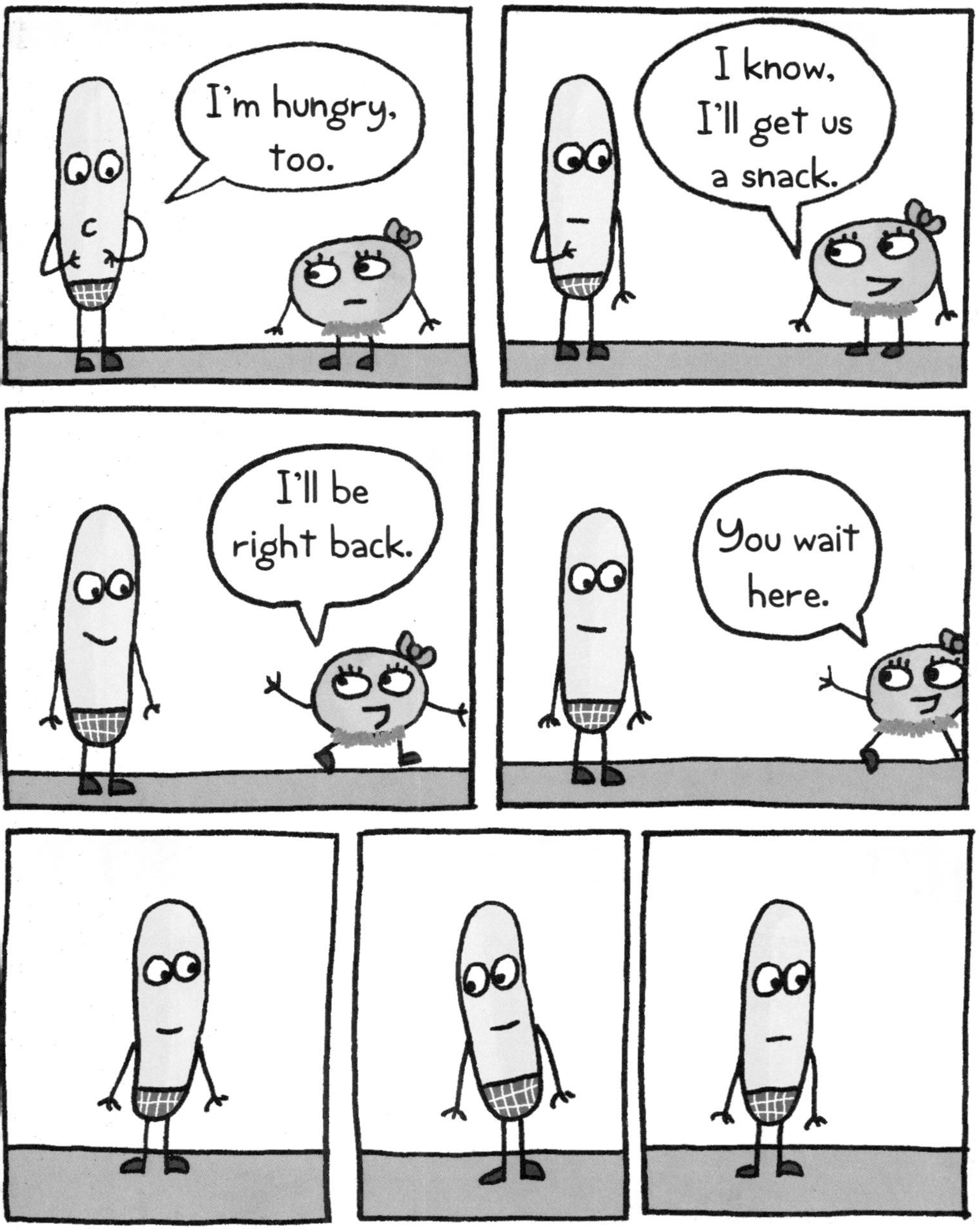
I'm hungry, too.
I know, I'll get us a snack.
I'll be right back.
You wait here.

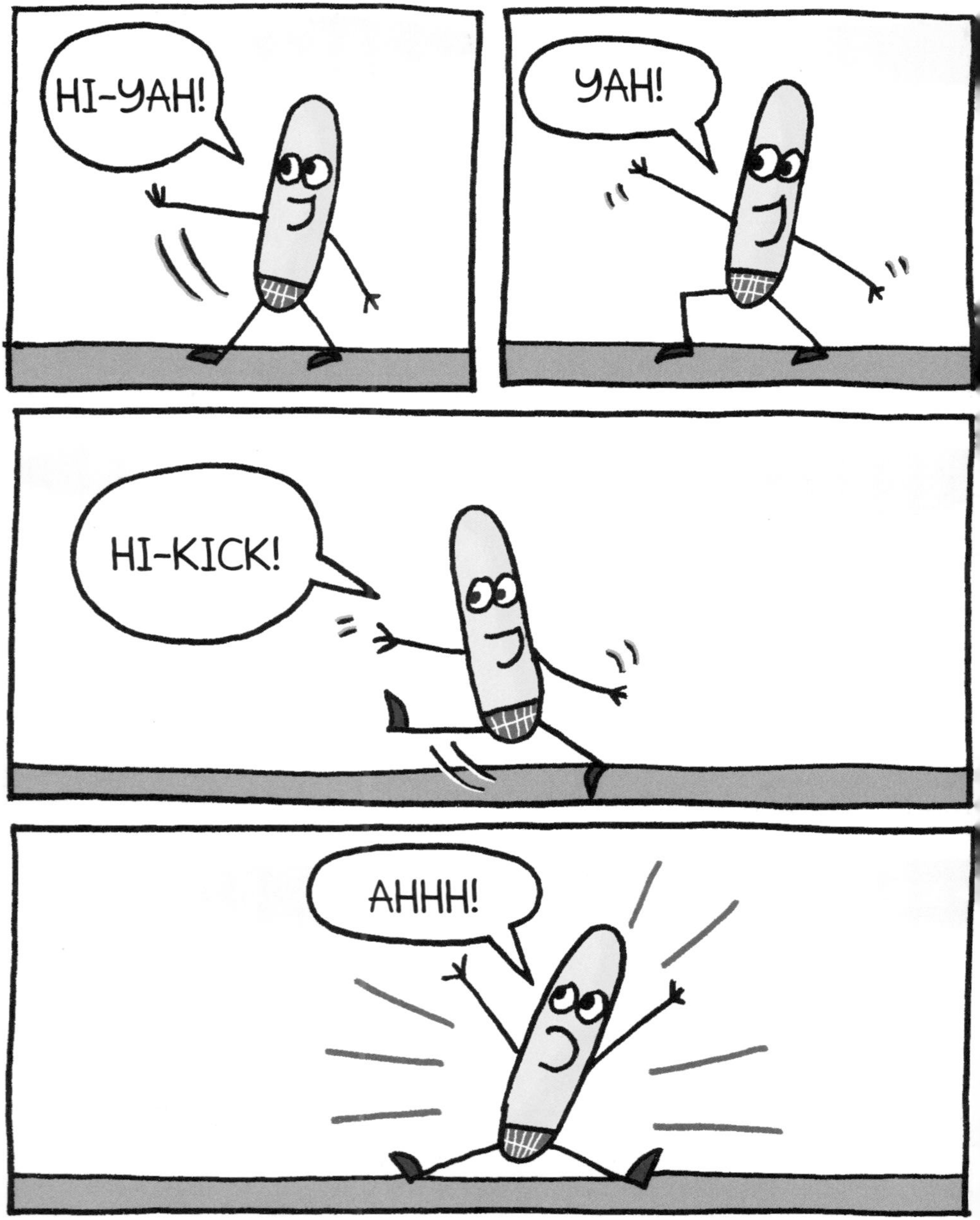
HI-YAH!
YAH!
HI-KICK!
AHHH!

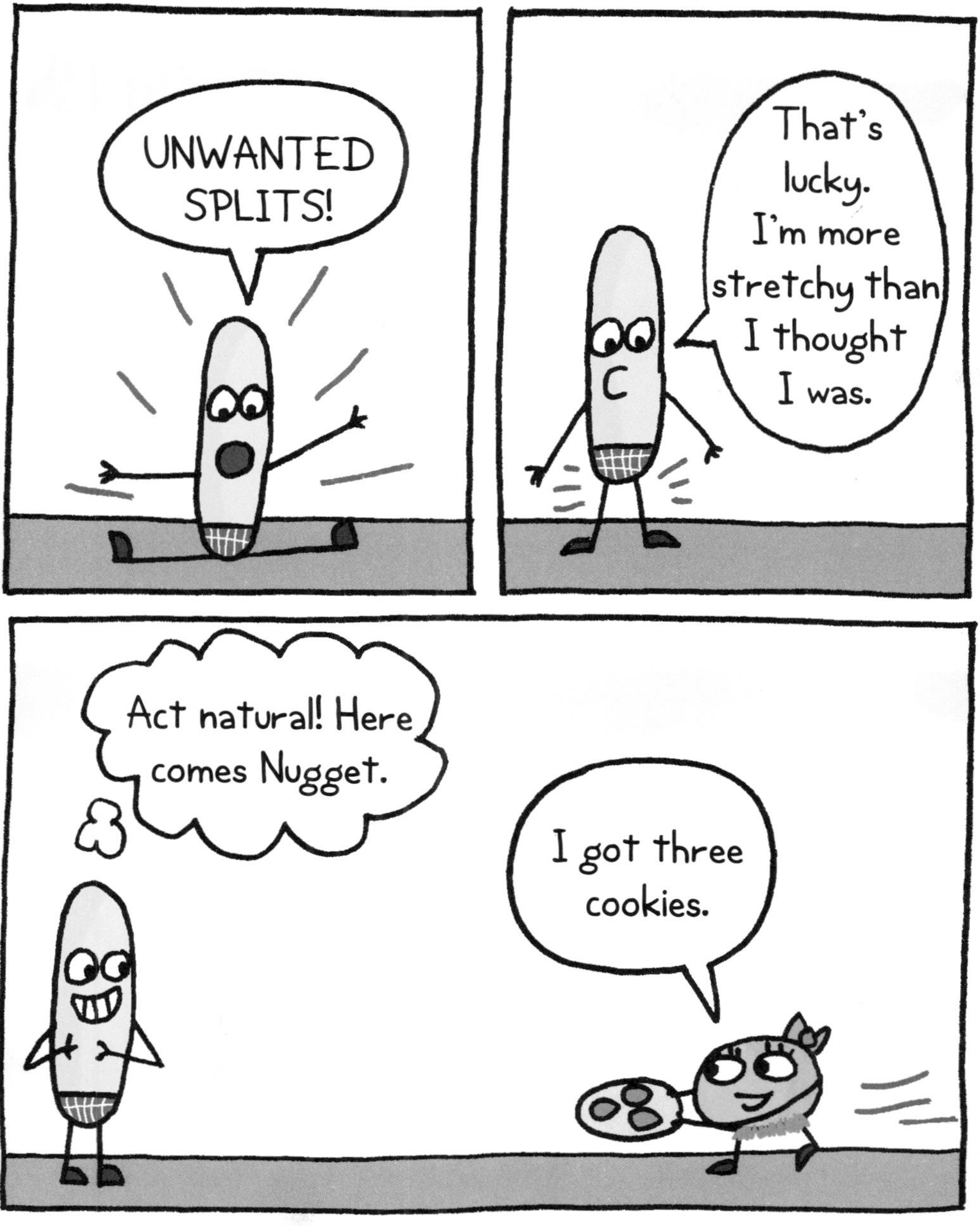
UNWANTED SPLITS!
That's lucky. I'm more stretchy than I thought I was.
Act natural! Here comes Nugget.
I got three cookies.

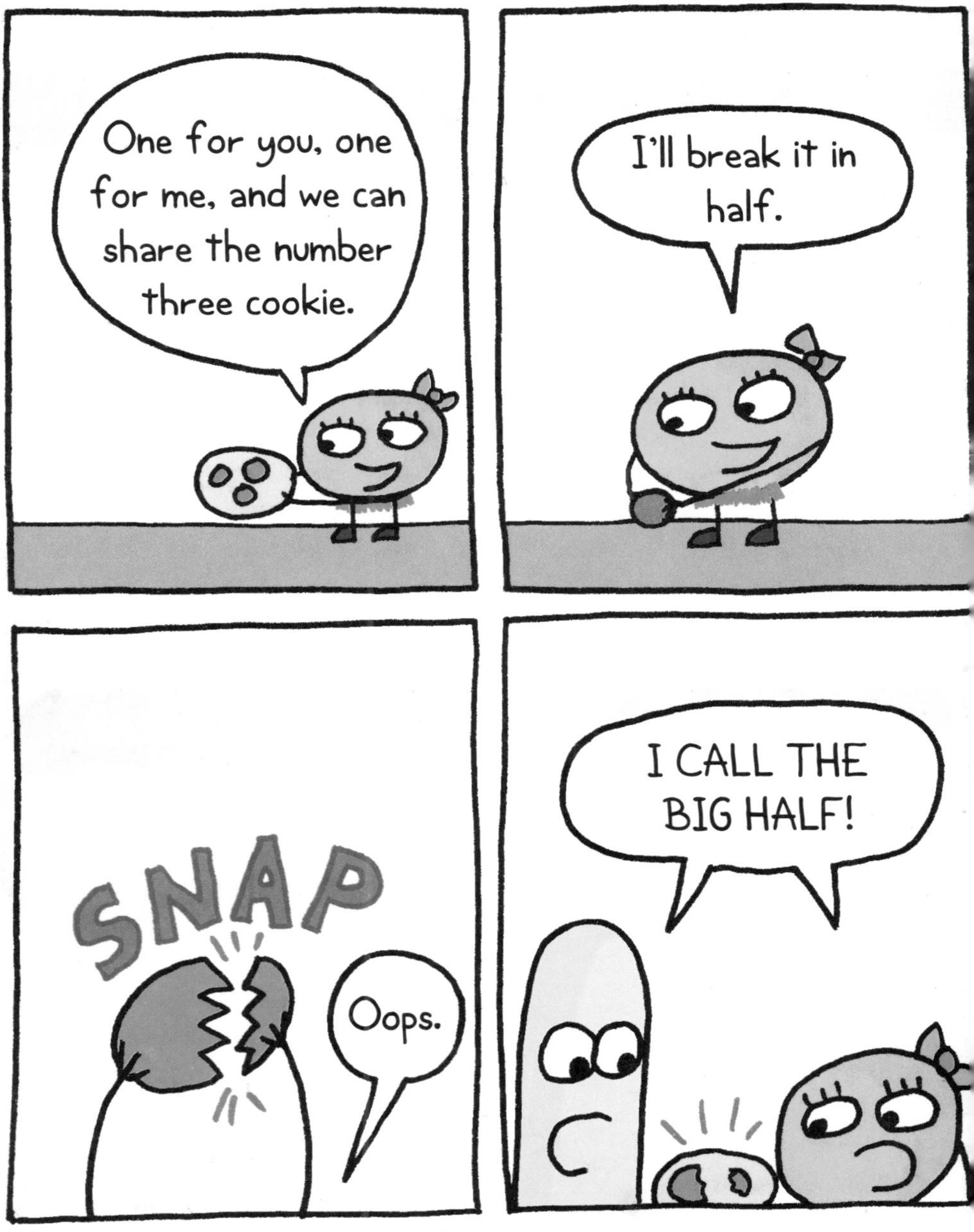
One for you, one for me, and we can share the number three cookie.
I'll break it in half.
SNAP
Oops.
I CALL THE BIG HALF!

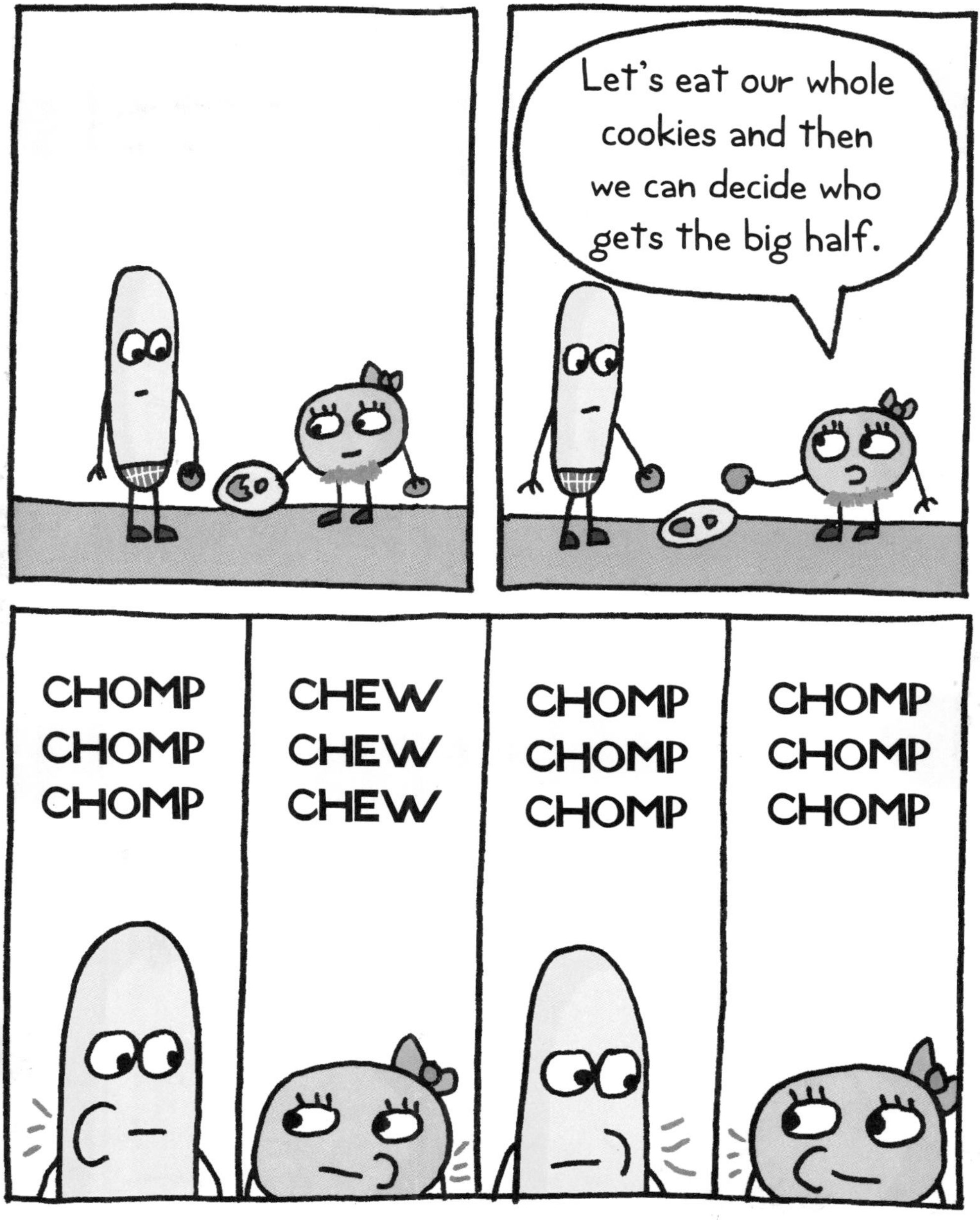
Let's eat our whole cookies and then we can decide who gets the big half.
CHOMP
CHOMP
CHOMP
CHEW
CHEW
CHEW
CHOMP
CHOMP
CHOMP
CHOMP
CHOMP
CHOMP

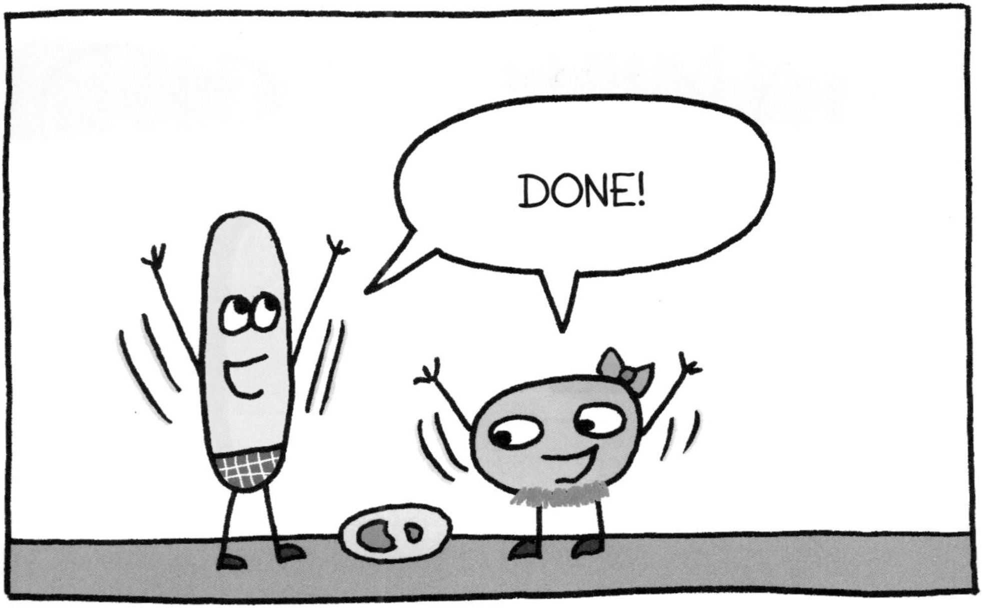
DONE!

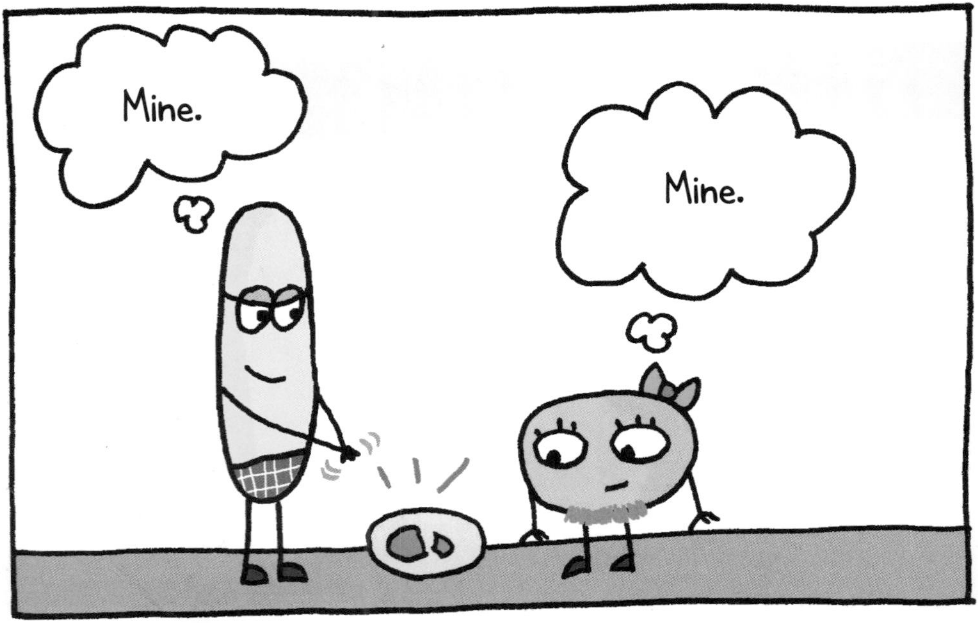
Mine.
Mine.

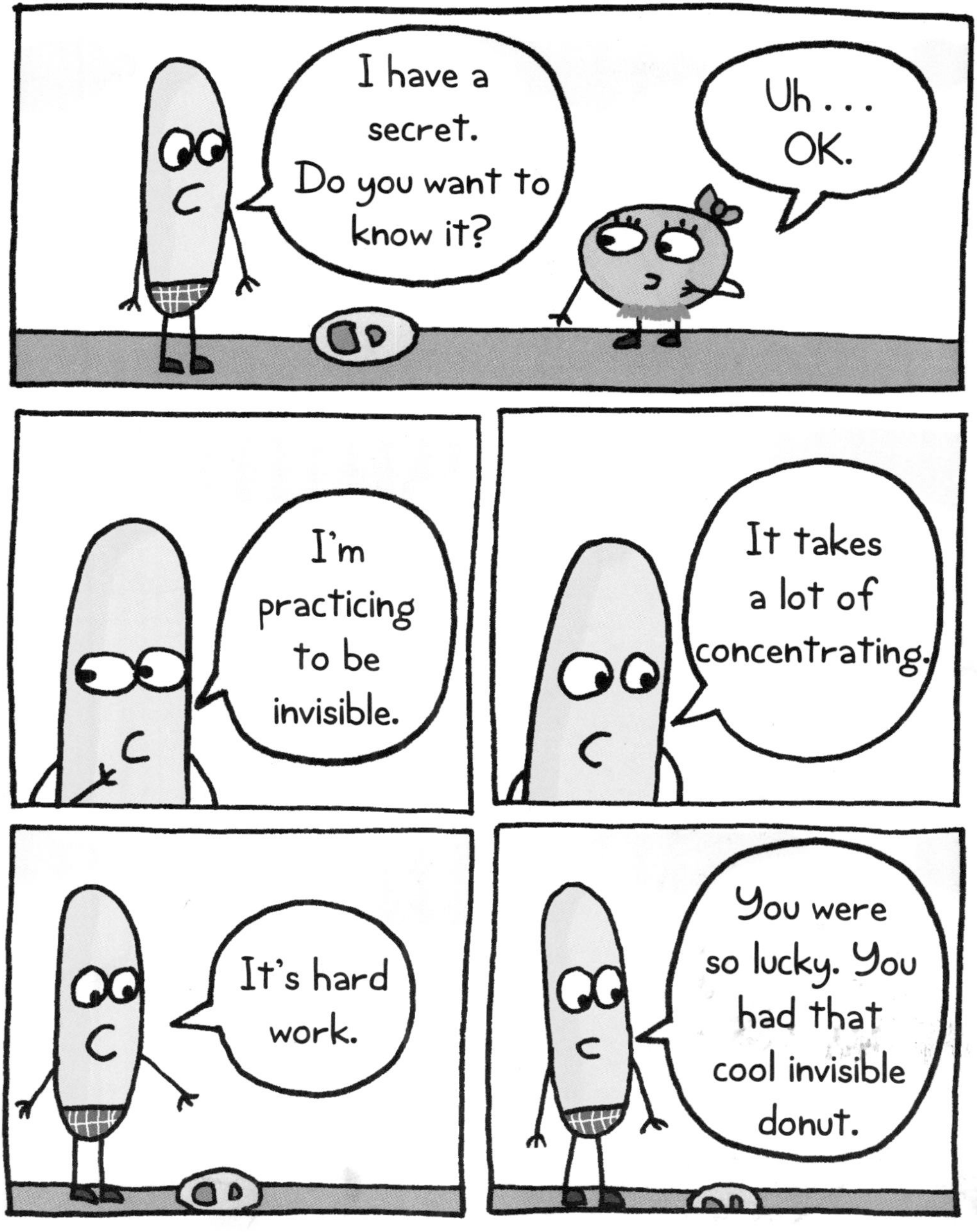
I have a secret. Do you want to know it?
Uh . . . OK.
I'm practicing to be invisible.
It takes a lot of concentrating.
It's hard work.
You were so lucky. You had that cool invisible donut.

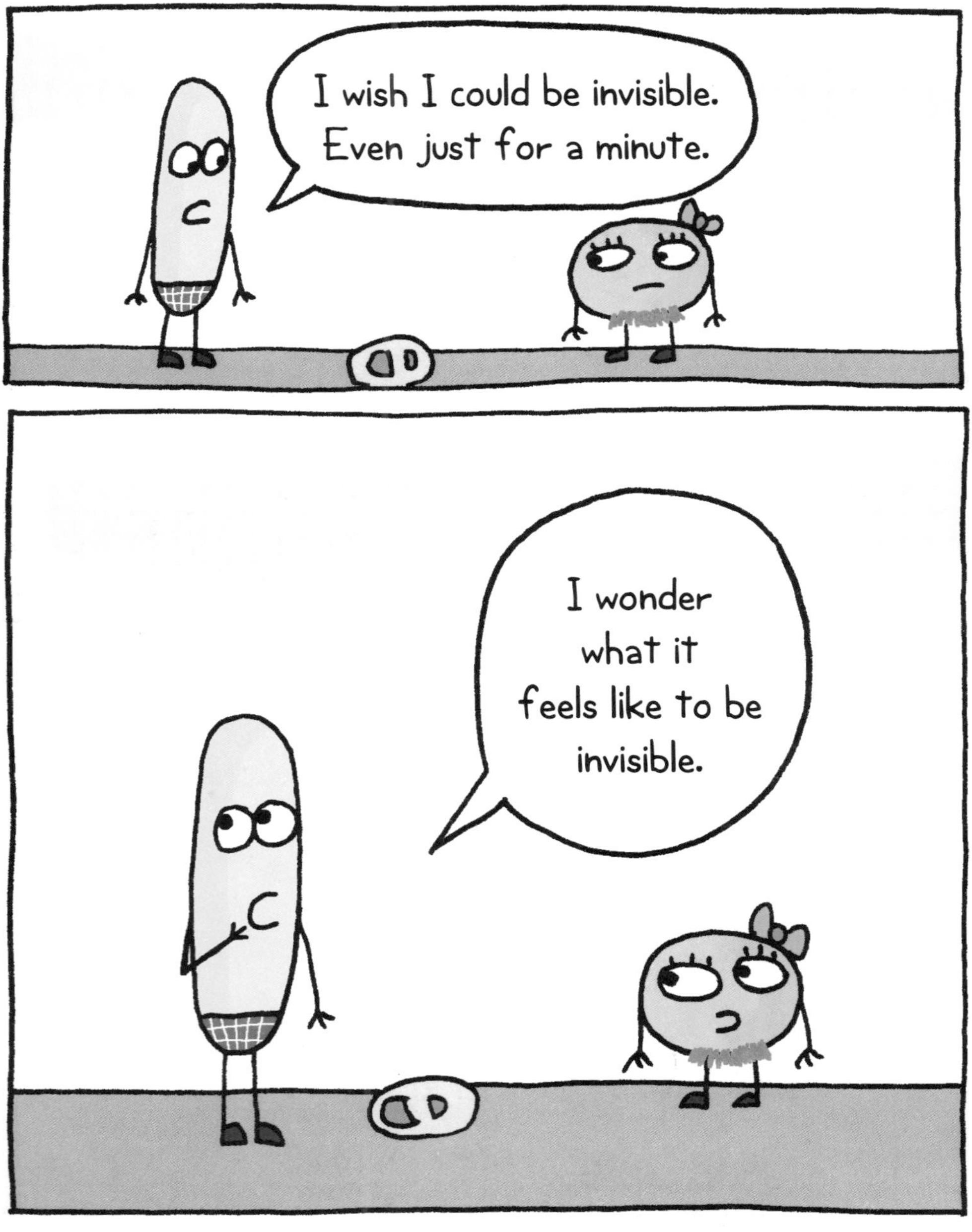
I wish I could be invisible.
Even just for a minute.
I wonder what it feels like to be invisible.

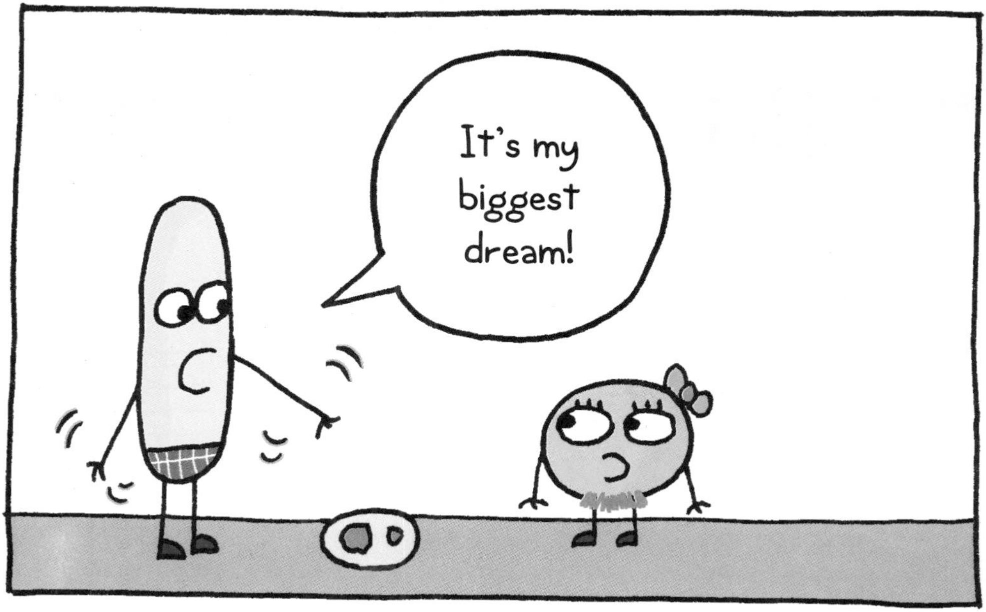
It's my
biggest
dream!

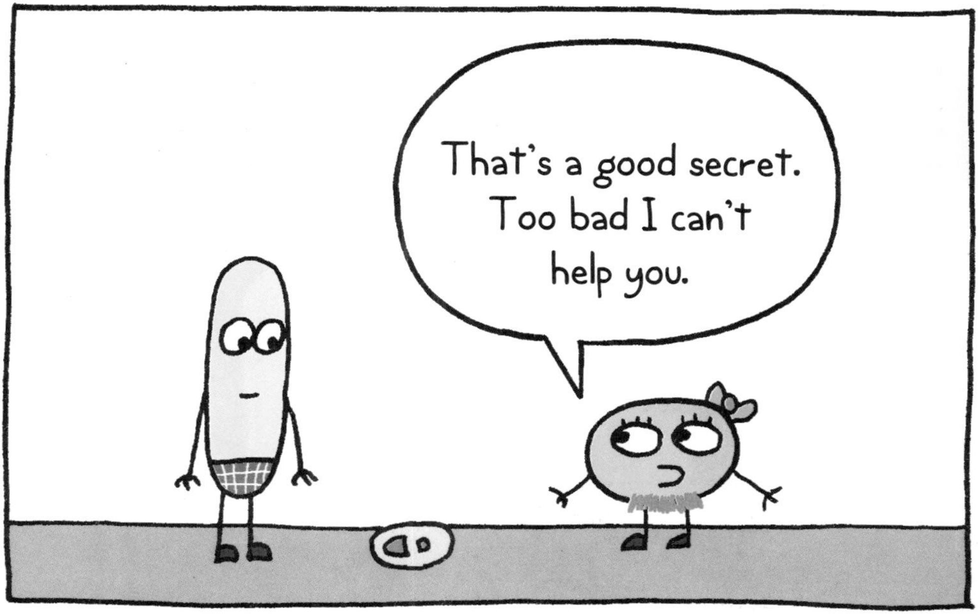
That's a good secret.
Too bad I can't
help you.

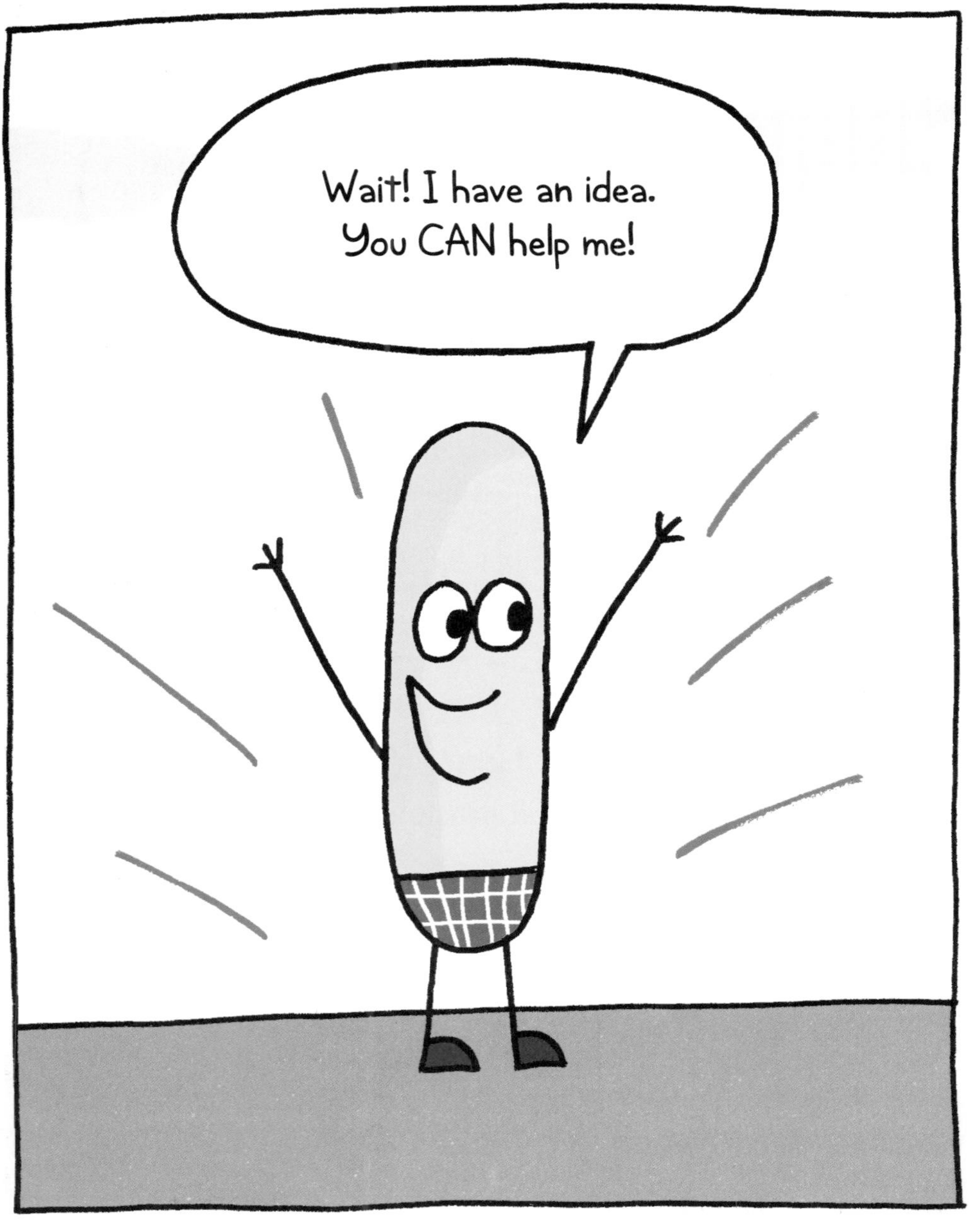
Wait! I have an idea.
You CAN help me!

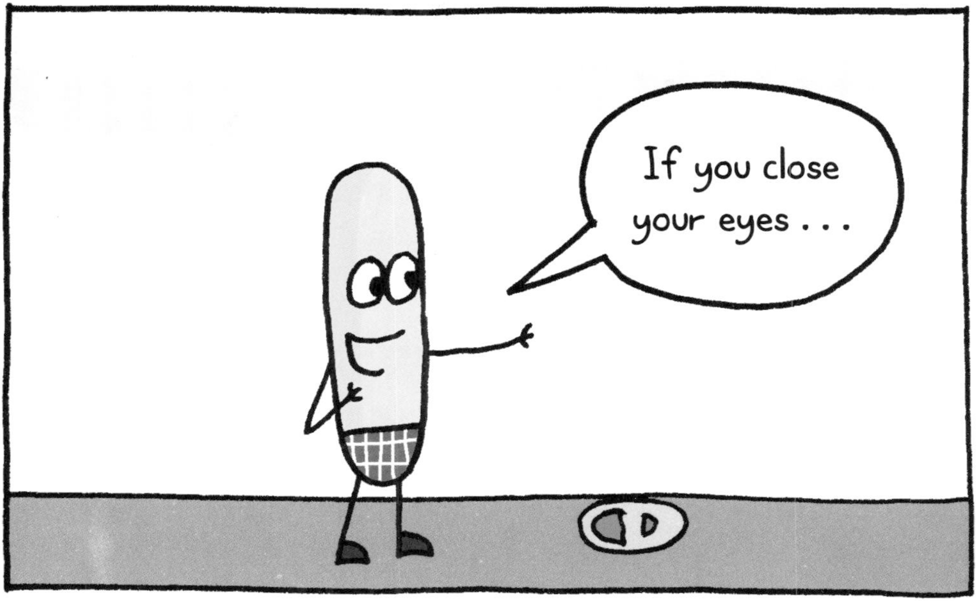
If you close your eyes . . .

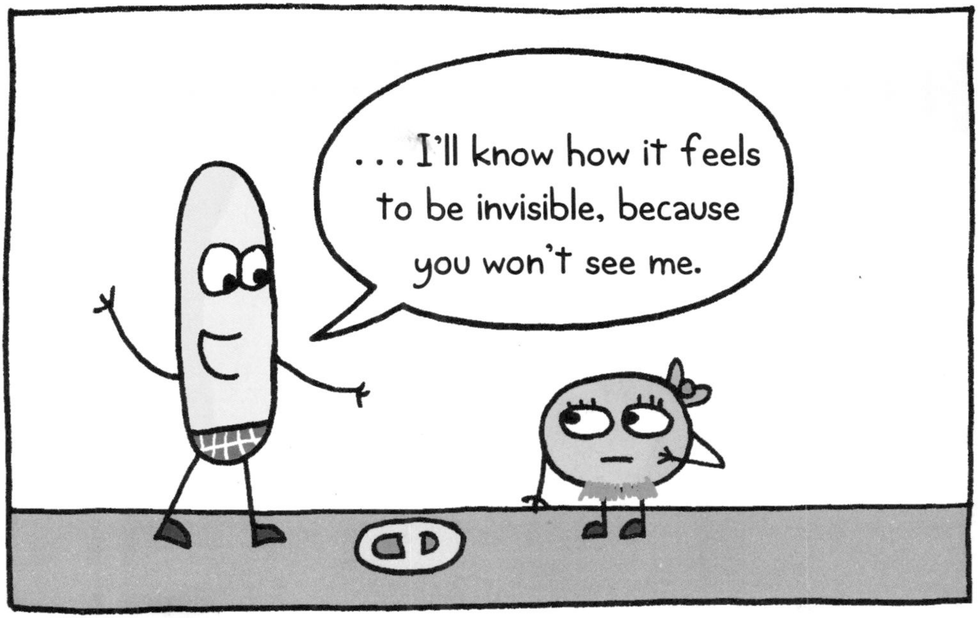
. . . I'll know how it feels to be invisible, because you won't see me.

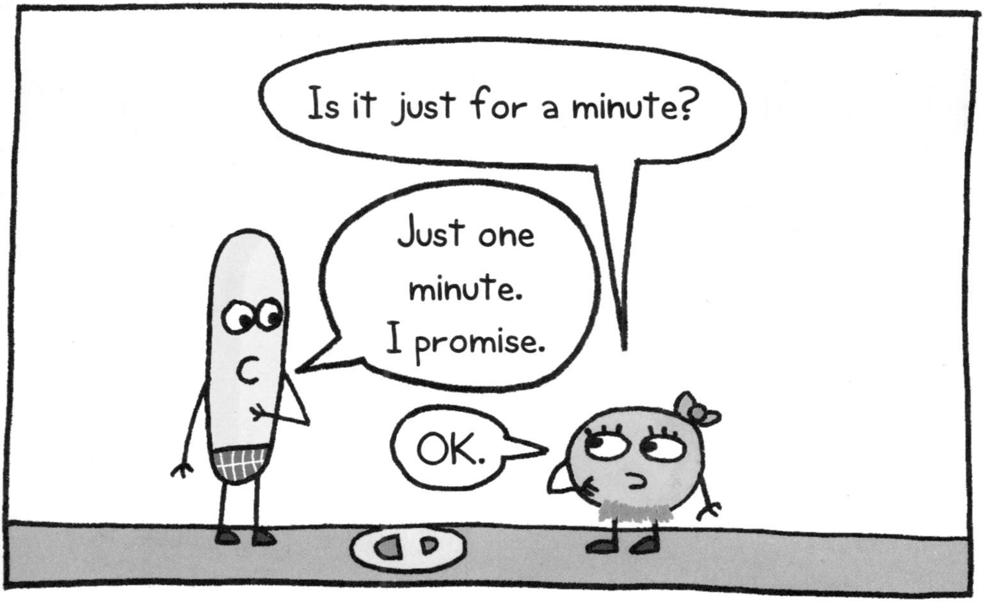
Is it just for a minute?
Just one minute. I promise.
OK.

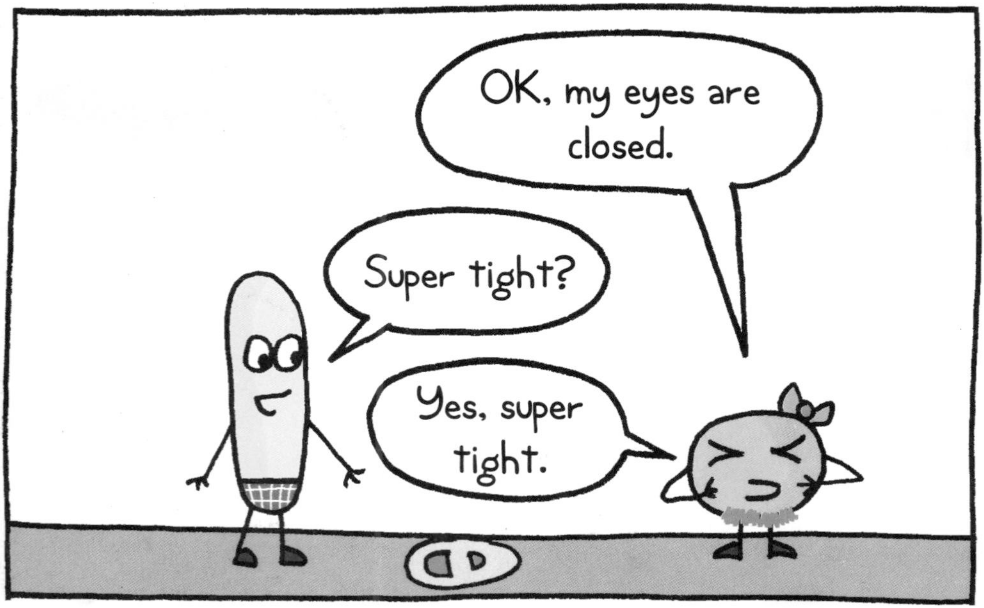
OK, my eyes are closed.
Super tight?
Yes, super tight.

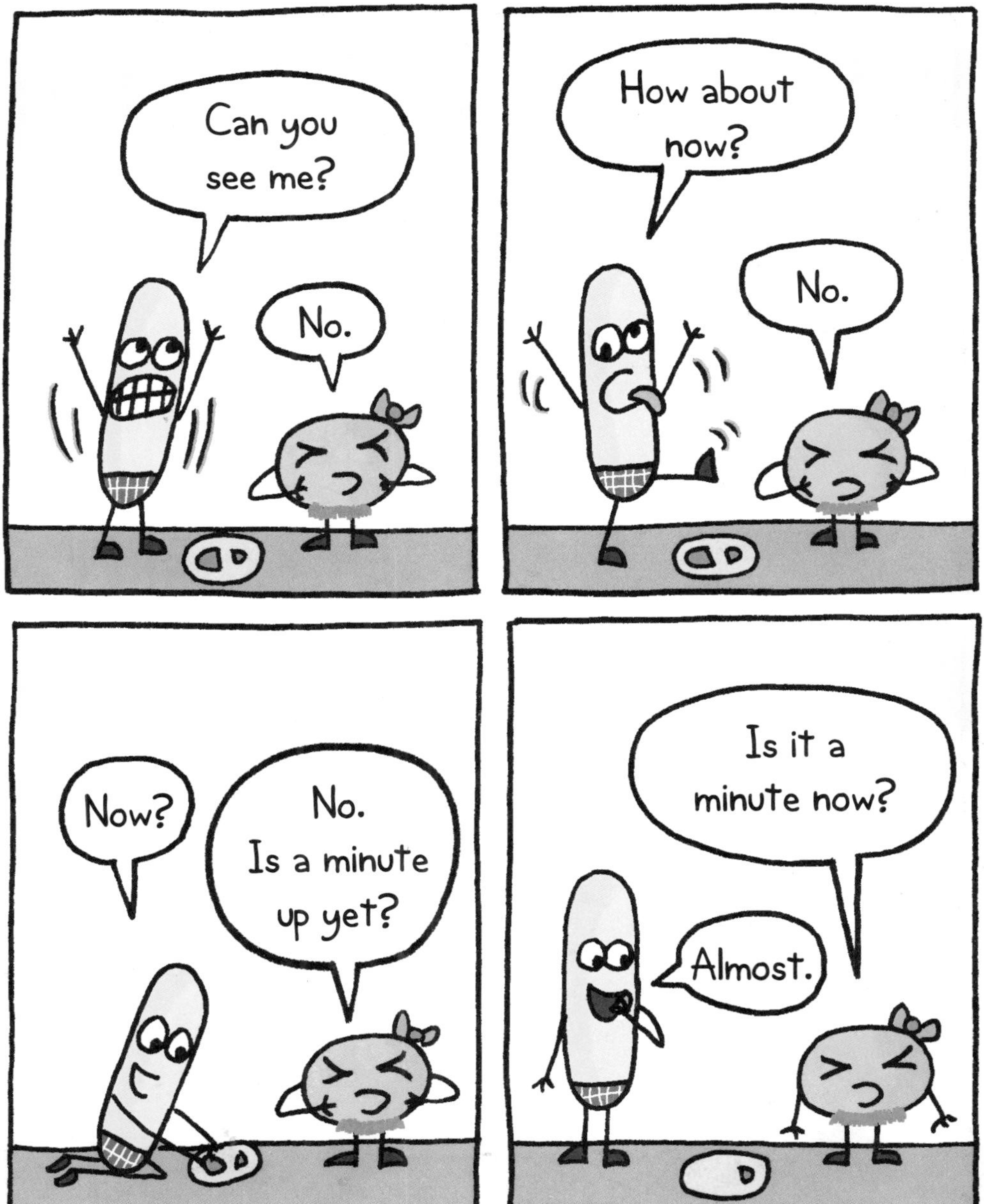
Can you see me?
No.
How about now?
No.
Now?
No. Is a minute up yet?
Is it a minute now?
Almost.

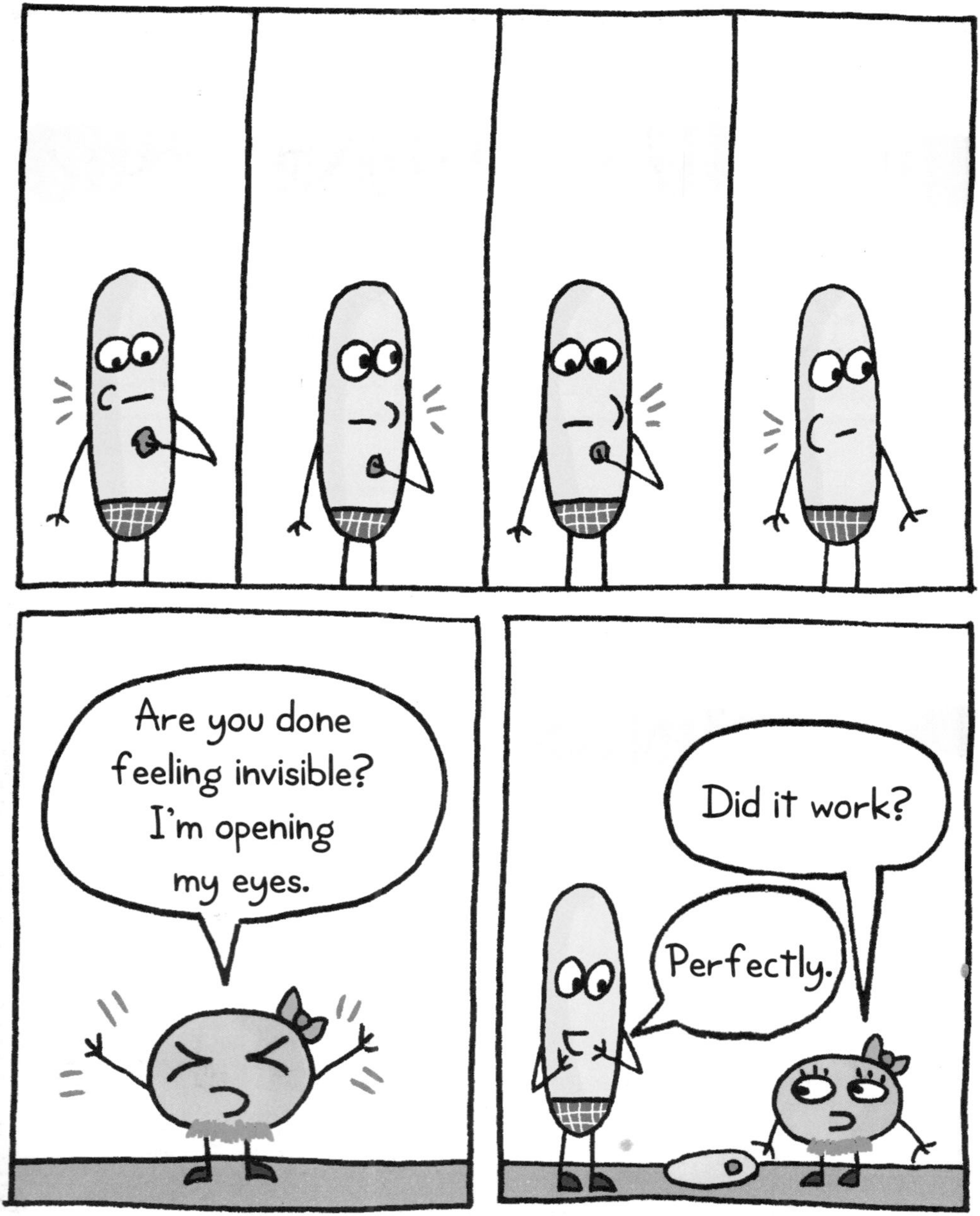
Are you done feeling invisible? I'm opening my eyes.
Did it work?
Perfectly.

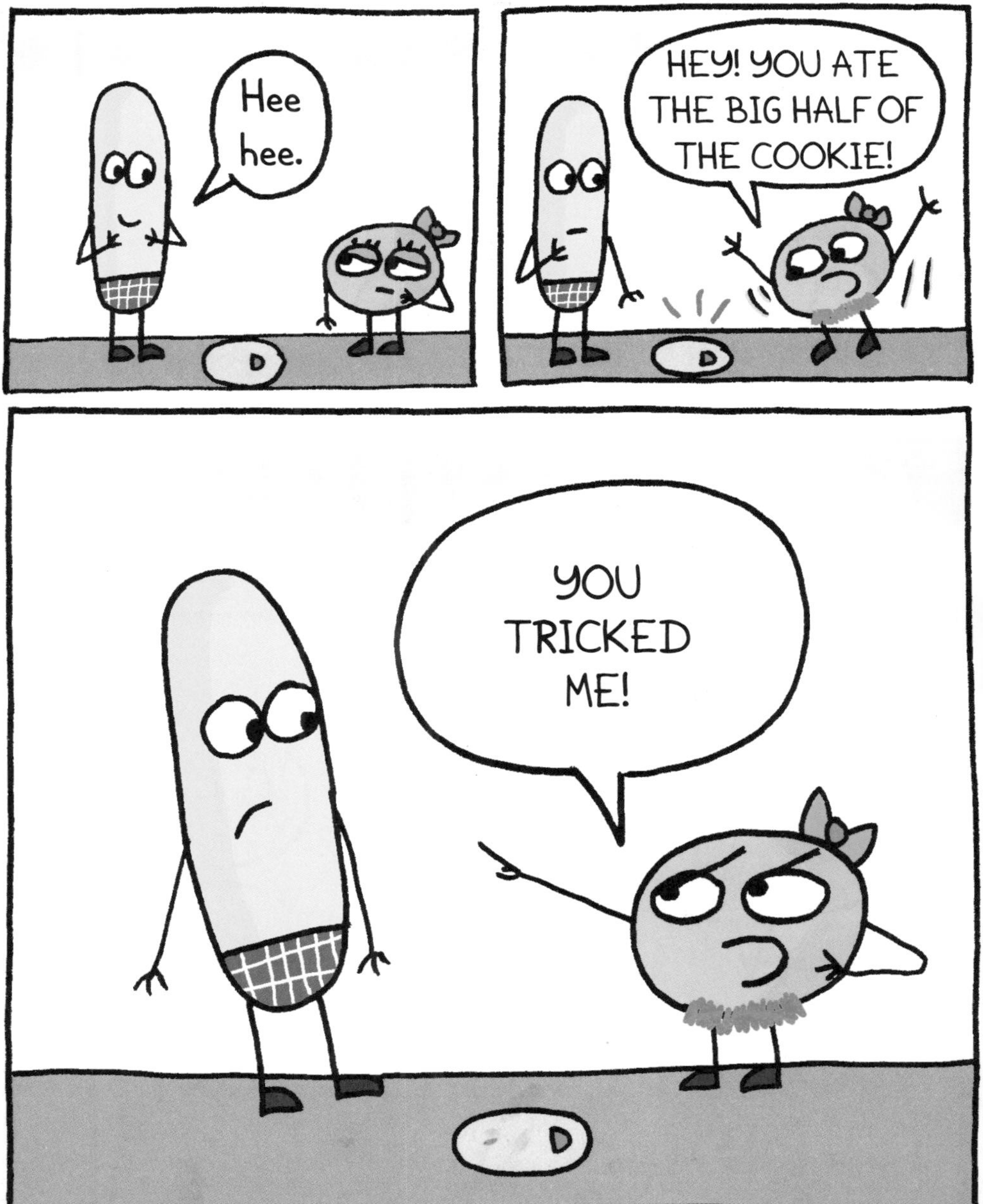
Hee hee.
HEY! YOU ATE THE BIG HALF OF THE COOKIE!
YOU TRICKED ME!

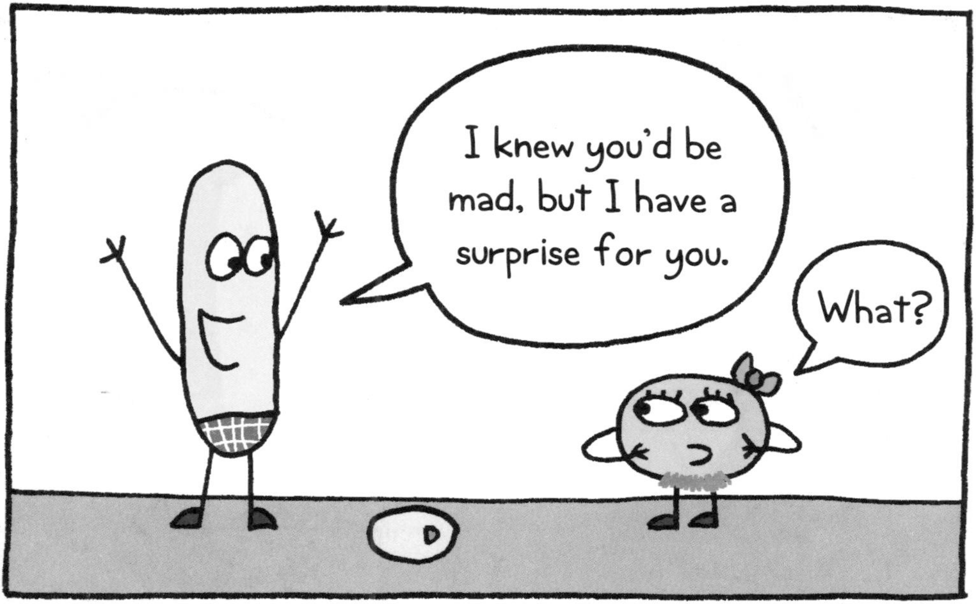
I knew you'd be mad, but I have a surprise for you.
What?

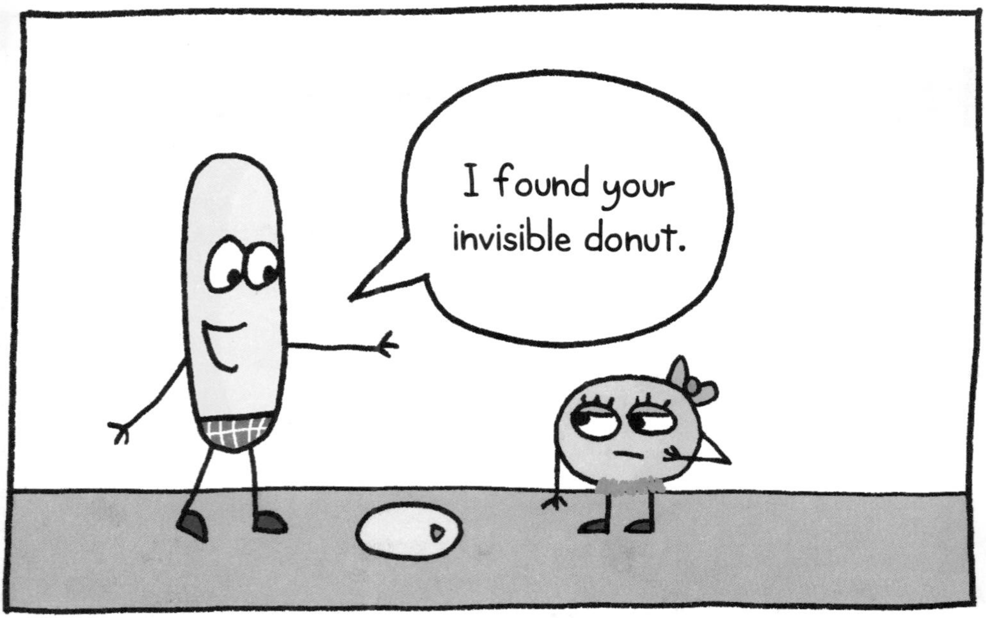
I found your invisible donut.

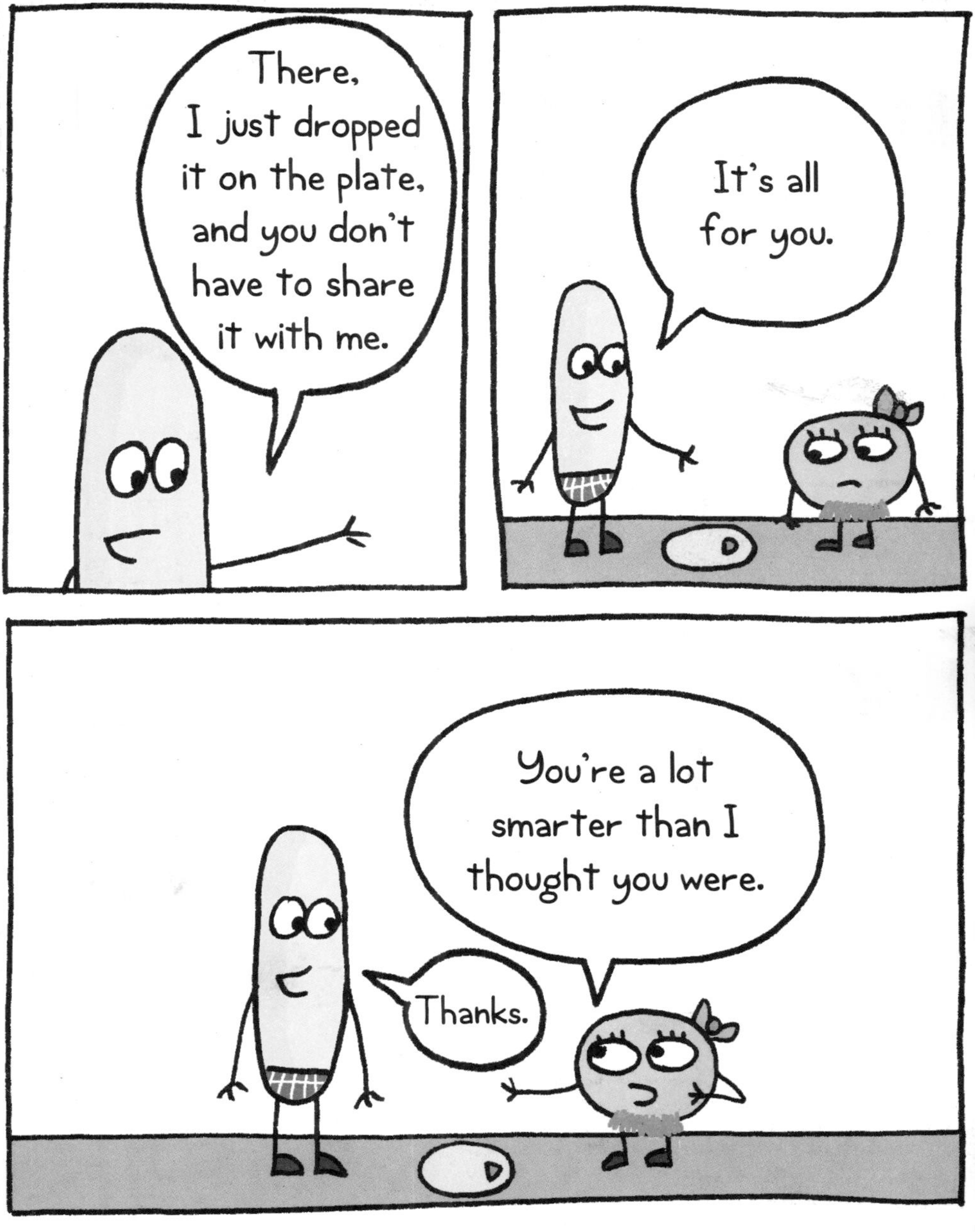
There, I just dropped it on the plate, and you don't have to share it with me.
It's all for you.
You're a lot smarter than I thought you were.
Thanks.

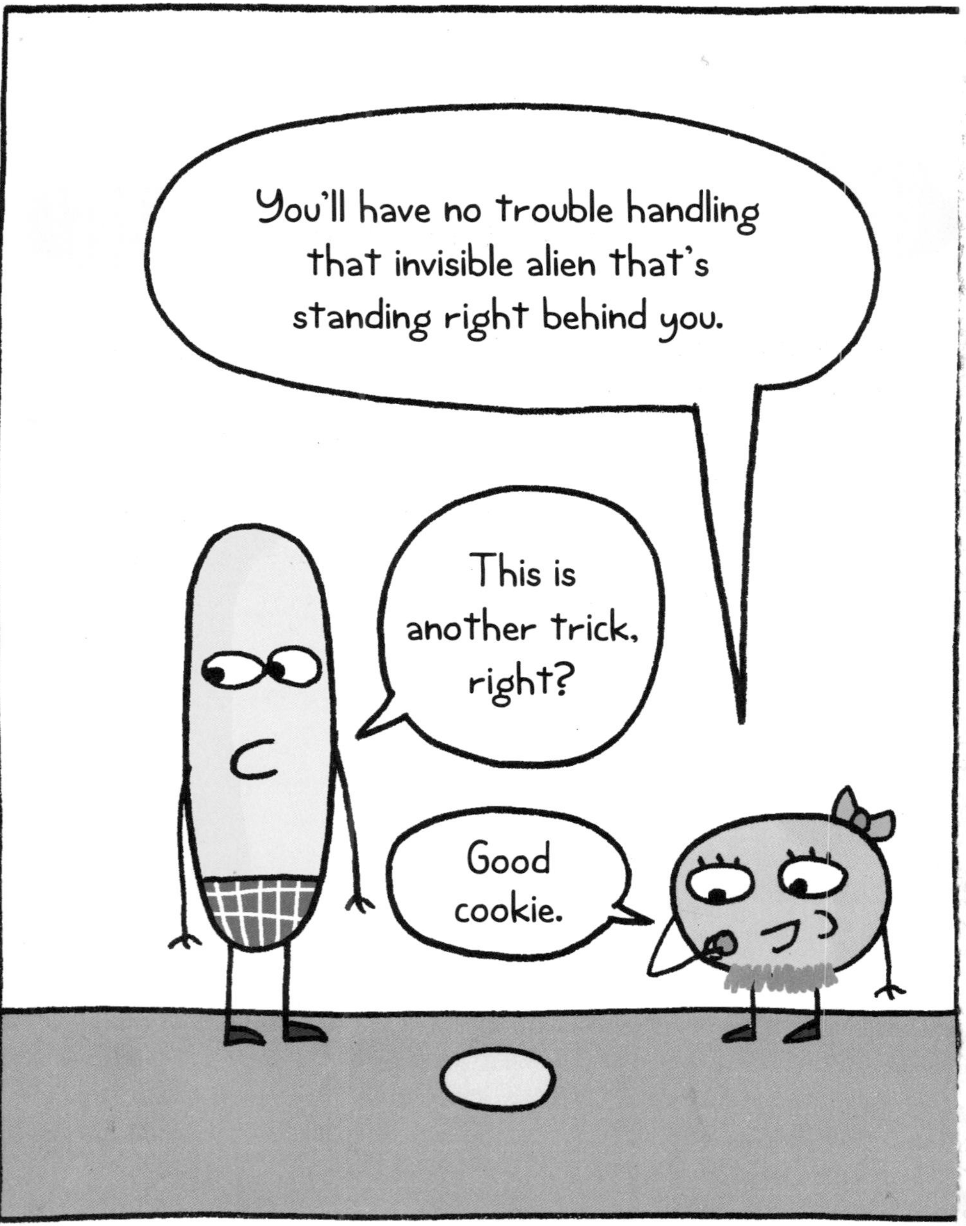
You'll have no trouble handling that invisible alien that's standing right behind you.
This is another trick, right?
Good cookie.